"EXTRAORDINARY...
This book could only have come from the pen of a writer who can't help being an enchanter."
Newsday

"COMPACT, RICH AND LASTING...
García Márquez is unquestionably the commanding colonel of the elite corps of Latin American writers... the story... is *performed*, like a mythical-anthropological ballet."
Chicago Sun-Times

"THE STORY IS COMICAL, HORRIFYING AND CURIOUSLY TENDER...
García Márquez launches himself at the impassivity of the South American heartland with a jeweler's toolbox. Working with precision, he assembles the grotesque, the hilarious and the surreal into a mosaic frieze carrying a message: silence, no change."
Los Angeles Times

"REMARKABLE, GRAPHIC, AND GRISLY...
about the impotent revenges of the impotent; about misdirected rage; about the heart blowing to bits from the burden of its own beat."
New York Magazine

Other Books in English Translation
BY GABRIEL GARCÍA MÁRQUEZ

NO ONE WRITES TO THE COLONEL AND STORIES

ONE HUNDRED YEARS OF SOLITUDE

THE AUTUMN OF THE PATRIARCH

INNOCENT ERÉNDIRA AND OTHER STORIES

IN EVIL HOURS

LEAF STORM AND OTHER STORIES

THE STORY OF A SHIPWRECKED SAILOR

CLANDESTINE IN CHILE: THE ADVENTUR MIGUEL LITTÍN

LOVE IN THE TIME OF CHOLERA

THE GENERAL IN HIS LABYRINTH

Chronicle of a Death Foretold

GABRIEL GARCÍA MÁRQUEZ

Translated from the Spanish by Gregory Rabassa

BALLANTINE BOOKS • NEW YORK

Originally published in Colombia as *Crónica de una muerte anunciada* by Editorial La Oveja Negra Ltda., Bogotá. Originally published in English in Great Britain by Jonathan Cape Ltd., London.

 Published in the United States of America by Ballantine Books, a division of Random House, Inc., New York,, and simultaneously in Canada by Random House of Canada Limited, Toronto.

Library of Congress Catalog Card Number: 82-48884

ISBN 0-345-31002-0

This edition published by arrangement with Alfred A. Knopf, Inc.

Manufactured in the United States of America

First Ballantine Books Edition: March 1984

OPM 38 37 36 35 34 33 32 31 30 29

the pursuit of love
is like falconry

GIL VICENTE

Chronicle of a Death Foretold

On the day they were going to kill him, Santiago Nasar got up at five-thirty in the morning to wait for the boat the bishop was coming on. He'd dreamed he was going through a grove of timber trees where a gentle drizzle was falling, and for an instant he was happy in his dream, but when he awoke he felt completely spattered with bird shit. "He was always dreaming about trees," Plácida Linero, his mother, told me twenty-seven years later, recalling the details of that distressing Monday. "The week before, he'd dreamed that he was alone in a tinfoil airplane and flying through the almond trees without bumping into anything," she said to me. She had a well-earned reputation as an accurate interpreter of other people's dreams, provided they were told her before eating, but she hadn't noticed any ominous augury in those two dreams of her son's, or in the other dreams of trees he'd described to her on the mornings preceding his death.

Nor did Santiago Nasar recognize the omen. He had slept little and poorly, without getting undressed, and he woke up with a headache and a sediment of copper stirrup on his palate, and he interpreted them as the natural havoc of the wedding revels that had gone on until after midnight. Furthermore: all the many people he ran into after leaving his house at five minutes past six and until he was carved up like a pig an hour later remembered him as being a little sleepy but in a good mood, and he remarked to all of them in a casual way that it was a very beautiful day. No one was certain if he was referring to the state of the weather. Many people coincided in recalling that it was a radiant morning with a sea breeze coming in through the banana groves, as was to be expected in a fine February of that period. But most agreed that the weather was funereal, with a cloudy, low sky and the thick smell of still waters, and that at the moment of the misfortune a thin drizzle was falling like the one Santiago Nasar had seen in his dream grove. I was recovering from the wedding revels in the apostolic lap of María Alejandrina Cervantes, and

I only awakened with the clamor of the alarm bells, thinking they had turned them loose in honor of the bishop.

Santiago Nasar put on a shirt and pants of white linen, both items unstarched, just like the ones he'd put on the day before for the wedding. It was his attire for special occasions. If it hadn't been for the bishop's arrival, he would have dressed in his khaki outfit and the riding boots he wore on Mondays to go to The Divine Face, the cattle ranch he'd inherited from his father and which he administered with very good judgment but without much luck. In the country he wore a .357 Magnum on his belt, and its armored bullets, according to what he said, could cut a horse in two through the middle. During the partridge season he would also carry his falconry equipment. In the closet he kept a Mannlicher Schoenauer .30-06 rifle, a .300 Holland & Holland Magnum rifle, a .22 Hornet with a double-powered telescopic sight, and a Winchester repeater. He always slept the way his father had slept, with the weapon hidden in the pillowcase, but before leaving the house that day he took out the bullets and put them in the drawer of the night table. "He never left it loaded," his mother told me. I knew that, and I also knew that he kept the guns in one place and hid the ammunition in another far removed so that nobody, not even casually, would yield to the temptation of loading them inside the house. It was a wise custom established by his father ever since one morning when a servant girl had shaken the case to get the pillow out and the pistol went off as it hit the floor and the bullet wrecked the cupboard in the room, went through the living room wall, passed through the dining room of the house next door with the thunder of war, and turned a life-size saint on the main altar of the church on the opposite side of the square to plaster dust. Santiago Nasar, who was a young child at the time, never forgot the lesson of that accident.

The last image his mother had of him was of his fleeting passage through the bedroom. He'd wakened her while he was feeling around trying to find an aspirin in the bathroom medicine chest, and she turned on the light and saw him appear in the doorway with a glass of water in his hand. So she would remember him forever. Santiago Nasar told her then about the dream, but she didn't pay any great attention to the trees.

"Any dream about birds means good health," she said.

She had watched him from the same hammock and in the same position in which I found her prostrated by the last lights of old age when I returned to this forgotten village, trying to put the broken mirror of memory back together from so many scattered shards. She could barely make out shapes in full light and had some medicinal leaves on her temples for the eternal headache that her son had left her the last time he went through the bedroom. She was on her side, clutching the cords at the head of the hammock as she tried to get up, and there in the half shadows was the baptistry smell that had startled me on the morning of the crime.

No sooner had I appeared on the threshold than she confused me with the memory of Santiago Nasar. "There he was," she told me. "He was dressed in white linen that had been washed in plain water because his skin was so delicate that it couldn't stand the noise of starch." She sat in the hammock for a long time, chewing pepper cress seeds, until the illusion that her son had returned left her. Then she sighed: "He was the man in my life."

I saw him in her memory. He had turned twenty-one the last week in January, and he was slim and pale and had his father's Arab eyelids and curly hair. He was the only child of a marriage of convenience without a single moment of happiness, but he seemed happy with his father until the latter died suddenly, three years before, and he continued seeming to be so with his solitary mother until the Monday of his death. From her he had inherited a sixth sense. From his father he learned at a very early age the manipulation of firearms, his love for horses, and the mastery of high-flying birds of prey, but from him he also learned the good arts of valor and prudence. They spoke Arabic between themselves, but not in front of Plácida Linero, so that she wouldn't feel excluded. They were never seen armed in town, and the only time they brought in their trained birds was for a demonstration of falconry at a charity bazaar. The death of his father had forced him to abandon his studies at the end of secondary school in order to take charge of the family ranch. By his nature, Santiago Nasar was merry and peaceful, and openhearted.

On the day they were going to kill him, his mother thought he'd got his days mixed up when she saw him dressed in white. "I reminded him that it was Monday," she told me. But he explained to her that he'd got dressed up pontifical style in case he had a chance to kiss the bishop's ring. She showed no sign of interest. "He won't even get off the boat," she told him. "He'll give an obligatory blessing, as always, and go back the way he came. He hates this town."

Santiago Nasar knew it was true, but church pomp had an irresistible fascination for him. "It's like the movies," he'd told me once. The only thing that interested his mother about the bishop's arrival, on the other hand, was for her son not to get soaked in the rain, since she'd heard him sneeze while he was sleeping. She advised him to take along an umbrella, but he waved good-bye and left the room. It was the last time she saw him.

Victoria Guzmán, the cook, was sure that it hadn't rained that day, or during the whole month of February. "On the contrary," she told me when I came to see her, a short time before her death. "The sun warms things up earlier than in August." She had been quartering three rabbits for lunch, surrounded by panting dogs, when Santiago Nasar entered the kitchen. "He always got up with the face of a bad night," Victoria Guzmán recalled without affection. Divina Flor, her daughter, who was just coming into bloom, served Santiago Nasar a mug of mountain coffee with a shot of cane liquor, as on every Monday, to help him bear the burden of the night before. The enormous kitchen, with the whispers from the fire and the hens sleeping on their perches, was breathing stealthily. Santiago Nasar swallowed another aspirin and sat down to drink the mug of coffee in slow sips, thinking just as slowly, without taking his eyes off the two women who were disemboweling the rabbits on the stove. In spite of her age, Victoria Guzmán was still in good shape. The girl, as yet a bit untamed, seemed overwhelmed by the drive of her glands. Santiago Nasar grabbed her by the wrist when she came to take the empty mug from him.

"The time has come for you to be tamed," he told her.

Victoria Guzmán showed him the bloody knife.

"Let go of her, white man," she ordered him seriously. "You won't have a drink of that water as long as I'm alive."

She'd been seduced by Ibrahim Nasar in the fullness of her adolescence. She'd made love to him in secret for several years in the stables of the ranch, and he brought her to be a house servant when the affection was over. Divina Flor, who was the daughter of a more recent mate, knew that she was destined for Santiago Nasar's furtive bed, and that idea brought out a premature anxiety in her. "Another man like that hasn't ever been born again," she told me, fat and faded and surrounded by the children of other loves. "He was just like his father," Victoria Guzmán answered her. "A shit." But she couldn't avoid a wave of fright as she remembered Santiago Nasar's horror when she pulled out the insides of a rabbit by the roots and threw the steaming guts to the dogs.

"Don't be a savage," he told her. "Make believe it was a human being."

Victoria Guzmán needed almost twenty years to understand that a man accustomed to killing defenseless animals could suddenly express such horror. "Good heavens," she explained with surprise. "All that was such a revelation." Nevertheless, she had so much repressed rage the morning of the crime that she went on feeding the dogs with the insides of the other rabbits, just to embitter Santiago Nasar's breakfast. That's what they were up to when the whole town awoke with the earthshaking bellow of the bishop's steamboat.

The house was a former warehouse, with two stories, walls of rough planks, and a peaked tin roof where the buzzards kept watch over the garbage on the docks. It had been built in the days when the river was so usable that many seagoing barges and even a few tall ships made their way up there through the marshes of the estuary. By the time Ibrahim Nasar arrived with the last Arabs at the end of the civil wars, seagoing ships no longer came there because of shifts in the river, and the warehouse was in disuse. Ibrahim Nasar bought it at a cheap price in order to set up an import store that he never did establish, and only when he was going to be married did he convert it into a house to live in. On the ground floor he opened up a parlor that served for everything, and in back he built a stable for four animals, the servants' quarters, and a country kitchen with windows opening onto the dock, through which the stench of the water came in at all hours. The only thing he left intact in the parlor was the spiral staircase rescued from some shipwreck. On the upper floor, where the customs offices had been before, he built two large bedrooms and five cubbyholes for the many children he intended having, and he constructed a wooden balcony that overlooked the almond trees on the square, where Plácida Linero would sit on March afternoons to console herself for her solitude. In the front he kept the main door and built two full-length windows with lathe-turned bars. He also kept the rear door, except a bit taller so that a horse could enter through it, and he kept a part of the old pier in use. That was always the door most used, not only because it was the natural entry to the mangers and the kitchen, but because it opened onto the street that led to the new docks without going through the square. The front door, except for festive occasions, remained closed and barred. Nevertheless, it was there, and not at the rear door, that the men who were going to kill him waited for Santiago Nasar, and it was through there that he went out to receive the bishop, despite the fact that he would have to walk completely around the house in order to reach the docks.

No one could understand such fatal coincidences. The investigating judge who came from Riohacha must have sensed them without daring to admit it, for his impulse to give them a rational explanation was obvious in his report. The door to the square was cited several times with a dime-novel title: "The Fatal Door." In reality, the only valid explanation seemed to be that of Plácida Linero, who answered the question with her mother wisdom: "My son never went out

the back door when he was dressed up." It seemed to be such an easy truth that the investigator wrote it down as a marginal note, but he didn't include it in the report.

Victoria Guzmán, for her part, had been categorical with her answer that neither she nor her daughter knew that the men were waiting for Santiago Nasar to kill him. But in the course of her years she admitted that both knew it when he came into the kitchen to have his coffee. They had been told it by a woman who had passed by after five o'clock to beg a bit of milk, and who in addition had revealed the motives and the place where they were waiting. "I didn't warn him because I thought it was drunkards' talk," she told me. Nevertheless, Divina Flor confessed to me on a later visit, after her mother had died, that the latter hadn't said anything to Santiago Nasar because in the depths of her heart she wanted them to kill him. She, on the other hand, didn't warn him because she was nothing but a frightened child at the time, incapable of a decision of her own, and she'd been all the more frightened when he grabbed her by the wrist with a hand that felt frozen and stony, like the hand of a dead man.

Santiago Nasar went through the shadowy

house with long strides, pursued by roars of jubilation from the bishop's boat. Divina Flor went ahead of him to open the door, trying not to have him get ahead of her among the cages of sleeping birds in the dining room, among the wicker furniture and the pots of ferns hanging down in the living room, but when she took the bar down, she couldn't avoid the butcher hawk hand again. "He grabbed my whole pussy," Divina Flor told me. "It was what he always did when he caught me alone in some corner of the house, but that day I didn't feel the usual surprise but an awful urge to cry." She drew away to let him go out, and through the half-open door she saw the almond trees on the square, snowy in the light of dawn, but she didn't have the courage to look at anything else. "Then the boat stopped tooting and the cocks began to crow," she told me. "It was such a great uproar that I couldn't believe there were so many roosters in town, and I thought they were coming on the bishop's boat." The only thing she could do for the man who had never been hers was leave the door unbarred, against Plácida Linero's orders, so that he could get back in, in case of emergency. Someone who was never identified had shoved an envelope under the door with a piece of paper warning Santiago Nasar that they were waiting for him to kill him, and, in addition, the note revealed the place, the motive, and other quite precise details of the plot. The message was on the floor when Santiago Nasar left home, but he didn't see it, nor did Divina Flor or anyone else until long after the crime had been consummated.

It had struck six and the street lights were still on. In the branches of the almond trees and on some balconies the colored wedding decorations were still hanging and one might have thought they'd just been hung in honor of the bishop. But the square, covered with paving stones up to the front steps of the church, where the bandstand was, looked like a trash heap, with empty bottles and all manner of debris from the public festivities. When Santiago Nasar left his house, several people were running toward the docks, hastened along by the bellowing of the boat.

The only place open on the square was a milk shop on one side of the church, where the two men were who were waiting for Santiago Nasar in order to kill him. Clotilde Armenta, the proprietress of the establishment, was the first to see him in the glow of dawn, and she had the impression that he was dressed in aluminum. "He already looked like a ghost," she told me. The men who were going to kill him had slept on the benches, clutching the knives wrapped in newspapers to their chests, and Clotilde Armenta held her breath so as not to awaken them.

They were twins: Pedro and Pablo Vicario. They were twenty-four years old, and they looked so much alike that it was difficult to tell them apart. "They were hard-looking, but of a good sort," the report said. I, who had known them since grammar school, would have written the same thing. That morning they were still wearing their dark wedding suits, too heavy and formal for the Caribbean, and they looked devastated by so many hours of bad living, but they'd done their duty and shaved. Although they hadn't stopped drinking since the eve of the wedding, they weren't drunk at the end of three days, but they looked, rather, like insomniac sleepwalkers. They'd fallen asleep with the first breezes of dawn, after almost three hours of waiting in Clotilde Armenta's store, and it was the first sleep they had had since Friday. They had barely awakened with the first bellow of the boat, but instinct awoke them completely when Santiago Nasar came out of his house. Then they both grabbed the rolled-up newspapers and Pedro Vicario started to get up.

"For the love of God," murmured Clotilde Armenta. "Leave him for later, if only out of respect for his grace the bishop."

"It was a breath of the Holy Spirit," she often repeated. Indeed, it had been a providential happening, but of momentary value only. When they heard her, the Vicario twins reflected, and the one who had stood up sat down again. Both followed Santiago Nasar with their eyes as he began to cross the square. "They looked at him more with pity," Clotilde Armenta said. At that moment the girls from the nuns' school crossed the square, trotting in disorder inside their orphans' uniforms.

Plácida Linero was right: the bishop didn't get off his boat. There were a lot of people at the dock in addition to the authorities and the schoolchildren, and everywhere one could see the crates of well-fattened roosters they were bearing as a gift for the bishop, because cockscomb soup was his favorite dish. At the pier there was so much firewood piled up that it would have taken at least two hours to load. But the boat didn't stop. It appeared at the bend in the river, snorting like a dragon, and then the band of musicians started to play the bishop's anthem, and the cocks began to crow in their baskets and aroused all the other roosters in town.

In those days the legendary paddle-wheelers that burned wood were on the point of disappearing, and the few that remained in service no longer had player pianos or bridal staterooms and were barely able to navigate against the current. But this one was new, and it had two smokestacks instead of one, with the flag painted on them like armbands, and the wheel made of planks at the stern gave it the drive of a seagoing ship. On the upper deck, beside the captain's cabin, was the bishop in his white cassock and with his retinue of Spaniards. "It was Christmas weather," my sister Margot said. What happened, according to her, was that the boat whistle let off a shower of compressed steam as it passed by the docks, and it soaked those who were closest to the edge. It was a fleeting illusion: the bishop began to make the sign of the cross in the air opposite the crowd on the pier, and he kept on doing it mechanically afterwards, without malice or inspiration, until the boat was lost from view and all that remained was the uproar of the roosters.

Santiago Nasar had reason to feel cheated. He had contributed several loads of wood to the public solicitudes of Father Carmen Amador, and in addition, he himself had chosen the capons with the most appetizing combs. But it was a passing annoyance. My sister Margot, who was with him on the pier, found him in a good mood and with an urge to go on with the festivities in spite of the fact that the aspirins had given him no relief. "He didn't seem to be chilly and was only thinking about what the wedding must have cost," she told me. Cristo Bedoya, who was with them, revealed figures that added to his surprise. He'd been carousing with Santiago Nasar and me until a little before four; he hadn't gone to sleep at his parents', but stayed chatting at his grandparents' house. There he obtained the bunch of figures that he needed to calculate what the party had cost. He recounted that they had sacrificed forty turkeys and eleven hogs for the guests, and four calves which the bridegroom had set up to be roasted for the people on the public square. He recounted that 205 cases of contraband alcohol had been consumed and almost two thousand bottles of cane liquor, which had been distributed among the crowd. There wasn't a single person, rich or poor, who hadn't participated in some way in the wildest party the town had ever seen. Santiago Nasar was dreaming aloud.

"That's what my wedding's going to be like," he said. "Life will be too short for people to tell about it."

My sister felt the angel pass by. She thought once more about the good fortune of Flora Miguel, who had so many things in life and was going to have Santiago Nasar as well on Christmas of that year. "I suddenly realized that there couldn't have been a better catch than him," she told me. "Just imagine: handsome, a man of his word, and with a fortune of his own at the age of twenty-one." She used to invite him to have breakfast at our house when there were manioc fritters, and my mother was making some that morning. Santiago Nasar accepted with enthusiasm.

"I'll change my clothes and catch up with you," he said, and he realized that he'd left his watch behind on the night table. "What time is it?"

It was six twenty-five. Santiago Nasar took Cristo Bedoya by the arm and led him toward the square.

"I'll be at your house inside of fifteen minutes," he told my sister.

She insisted that they go together right away because breakfast was already made. "It was a strange insistence," Cristo Bedoya told me. "So much so that sometimes I've thought that Margot already knew that they were going to kill him and wanted to hide him in your house." Santiago Nasar persuaded her to go on ahead while he put on his riding clothes, because he had to be at The Divine Face early in order to geld some calves. He took leave of her with the same wave with which he'd said good-bye to his mother and went off toward the square on the arm of Cristo Bedoya. It was the last time she saw him.

Many of those who were on the docks knew that they were going to kill Santiago Nasar. Don Lázaro Aponte, a colonel from the academy making use of his good retirement, and town mayor for eleven years, waved to him with his fingers. "I had my own very real reasons for believing he wasn't in any danger anymore," he told me. Father Carmen Amador wasn't worried either. "When I saw him safe and sound I thought it had all been a fib," he told me. No one even wondered whether Santiago Nasar had been warned, because it seemed impossible to all that he hadn't.

In reality, my sister Margot was one of the few people who still didn't know that they were going to kill him. "If I'd known, I would have taken him home with me even if I had to hog-tie him," she declared to the investigator. It was strange that she hadn't known, but it was even stranger that my mother didn't know either, because she knew about everything before anyone else in the house, in spite of the fact that she hadn't gone out into the street in years, not even to attend mass. I had become aware of that quality of hers ever since I began to get up early for school. I would find her the way she was in those days, pale and stealthy, sweeping the courtyard with a homemade broom in the ashen glow of dawn, and between sips of coffee she would proceed to tell me what had happened in the world while we'd been asleep. She seemed to have secret threads of communication with the other people in town, especially those her age, and sometimes she would surprise us with news so ahead of its time that she could only have known it through powers of divination. That morning, however, she didn't feel the throb of the tragedy that had been gestating since three o'clock. She'd finished sweeping the courtyard, and when my sister Margot went out to meet the bishop she found her grinding manioc for the fritters. "Cocks could be heard," my mother is accustomed to saying, remembering that day. She never associated the distant uproar with the arrival of the bishop, however, but with the last leftovers from the wedding.

Our house was a good distance from the main square, in a mango grove on the river. My sister Margot had gone to the docks by walking along the shore, and the people were too excited with the bishop's visit to worry about any other news. They'd placed the sick people in the archways to receive God's medicine, and women came running out of their yards with turkeys and suckling pigs and all manner of things to eat, and from the opposite shore came canoes bedecked with flowers. But after the bishop passed without setting foot on land, the other repressed news assumed its scandalous dimensions. Then it was that my sister Margot learned about it in a thorough and brutal way: Angela Vicario, the beautiful girl who'd gotten married the day before, had been returned to the house of her parents, because her husband had discovered that she wasn't a virgin. "I felt that I was the one who was going to die," my sister said. "But no matter how much they tossed the story back and forth, no one could explain to me how poor Santiago Nasar ended up being involved in such a mix-up." The only thing they knew for sure was that Angela Vicario's brothers were waiting for him to kill him.

My sister returned home gnawing at herself inside to keep from crying. She found my mother in the dining room, wearing a Sunday dress with blue flowers that she had put on in case the bishop came by to pay us a call, and she was singing the fado about invisible love as she set the table. My sister noted that there was one more place than usual.

"It's for Santiago Nasar," my mother said. "They told me you'd invited him for breakfast."

"Take it away," my sister said.

Then she told her. "But it was as if she already knew," she said to me. "It was the same as always: you begin telling her something and before the story is half over she already knows how it came out." That bad news represented a knotty problem for my mother. Santiago Nasar had been named for her and she was his godmother when he was christened, but she was also a blood relative of Pura Vicario, the mother of the returned bride. Nevertheless, no sooner had she heard the news than she put on her high-heeled shoes and the church shawl she only wore for visits of condolence. My father, who had heard everything from his bed, appeared in the dining room in his pajamas and asked in alarm where she was going.

"To warn my dear friend Plácida," she answered. "It isn't right that everybody should know that they're going to kill her son and she the only one who doesn't."

"We've got the same ties to the Vicarios that we do with her," my father said.

"You always have to take the side of the dead," she said.

My younger brothers began to come out of the other bedrooms. The smallest, touched by the breath of tragedy, began to weep. My mother paid no attention to them; for once in her life she didn't even pay any attention to her husband.

"Wait a minute and I'll get dressed," he told her.

She was already in the street. My brother Jaime, who wasn't more than seven at the time, was the only one who was dressed for school.

"You go with her," my father ordered.

Jaime ran after her without knowing what was happening or where they were going, and grabbed her hand. "She was going along talking to herself," Jaime told me. "Lowlifes," she was saying under her breath, "shitty animals that can't do anything that isn't something awful." She didn't even realize that she was holding the child by the hand. "They must have thought I'd gone crazy," she told me. "The only thing I can remember is that in the distance you could hear the noise of a lot of people, as if the wedding party had started up again, and everybody was running toward the square." She quickened her step, with the determination she was capable of when there was a life at stake, until somebody who was running in the opposite direction took pity on her madness.

"Don't bother yourself, Luisa Santiaga," he shouted as he went by. "They've already killed him."

BAYARDO SAN ROMÁN, THE MAN WHO had given back his bride, had turned up for the first time in August of the year before: six months before the wedding. He arrived on the weekly boat with some saddlebags decorated with silver that matched the buckle of his belt and the rings on his boots. He was around thirty years old, but they were well-concealed, because he had the waist of a novice bullfighter, golden eyes, and a skin slowly roasted by saltpeter. He arrived wearing a short jacket and very tight trousers, both of natural calfskin, and kid gloves of the same color. Magdalena Oliver had been with him on the boat and couldn't take her eyes off him during the whole trip. "He looked like a fairy," she told me. "And it was a pity, because I could have buttered him and eaten him alive." She wasn't the only one who thought so, nor was she the last to realize that Bayardo San Román was not a man to be known at first sight.

My mother wrote to me at school toward the end of August and said in a casual postscript: "A very strange man has come." In the following letter she told me: "The strange man is called Bayardo San Román, and everybody says he's enchanting, but I haven't seen him." Nobody knew what he'd come for. Someone who couldn't resist the temptation of asking him, a little before the wedding, received the answer: "I've been going from town to town looking for someone to marry." It might have been true, but he would have answered anything else in the same way, because he had a way of speaking that served to conceal rather than to reveal.

The night he arrived he gave them to understand at the movies that he was a track engineer, and spoke of the urgency for building a railroad into the interior so that we could keep ahead of the river's fickle ways. On the following day he had to send a telegram and he transmitted it on the key himself, and in addition, he taught the telegrapher a formula of his so that he could keep on using the worn-out batteries. With the same assurance he talked about frontier illnesses with a military doctor who had come through during those months of conscription. He liked noisy and long-lasting festivities, but he was a good drinker, a mediator of fights, and an enemy of cardsharps. One Sunday after mass he challenged the most skillful swimmers, who were many, and left the best behind by twenty strokes in crossing the river and back. My mother told me about it in a letter, and at the end she made a comment that was very much like her: "It also seems that he's swimming in gold." That was in reply to the premature legend that Bayardo San Román not only was capable of doing everything, and doing it quite well, but also had access to endless resources.

My mother gave him the final blessing in a letter in October: "People like him a lot," she told me, "because he's honest and has a good heart, and last Sunday he received communion on his knees and helped with the mass in Latin." In those days it wasn't permitted to receive communion standing and everything was in Latin, but my mother is accustomed to noting that kind of superfluous detail when she wants to get to the heart of the matter. Nevertheless, after that consecrated verdict she wrote me two letters in which she didn't say anything about Bayardo San Román, not even when it was known very well that he wanted to marry Angela Vicario. Only a long time after the unfortunate wedding did she confess to me that she actually knew him when it was already too late to correct the October letter, and that his golden eyes had caused the shudder of a fear in her.

"He reminded me of the devil," she told me, "but you yourself had told me that things like that shouldn't be put into writing."

I met him a short while after she did, when I came home for Christmas vacation, and I found him just as strange as they had said. He seemed attractive, certainly, but far from Magdalena Oliver's idyllic vision. He seemed more serious to me than his antics would have led one to believe, and with a hidden tension that was barely concealed by his excessive good manners. But above all, he seemed to me like a very sad man. At that time he had already formalized his contract of love with Angela Vicario.

It had never been too well-established how they had met. The landlady of the bachelors' boardinghouse where Bayardo San Román lived told of how he'd been napping in a rocking chair in the parlor toward the end of September, when Angela Vicario and her mother crossed the square carrying two baskets of artificial flowers. Bayardo San Román half-awoke, saw the two women dressed in the unforgiving black worn by the only living creatures in the morass of two o'clock in the afternoon, and asked who the young one was. The landlady answered him that she was the youngest daughter of the woman with her and that her name was Angela Vicario. Bayardo San Román followed them with his look to the other side of the square.

"She's well-named," he said.

Then he rested his head on the back of the rocker and closed his eyes again.

"When I wake up," he said, "remind me that I'm going to marry her."

Angela Vicario told me that the landlady of the boardinghouse had spoken to her about that occurrence before Bayardo San Román began courting her. "I was quite startled," she told me. Three people who had been in the boardinghouse confirmed that it had taken place, but four others weren't sure. On the other hand, all the versions agreed that Angela Vicario and Bayardo San Román had seen each other for the first time on the national holiday in October during a charity bazaar at which she was in charge of singing out the raffle numbers. Bayardo San Román came to the bazaar and went straight to the booth run by the languid raffler, who was in mourning, and he asked her the price of the music box inlaid with mother-of-pearl that must have been the major attraction of the fair. She answered him that it was not for sale but was to be raffled off.

"So much the better," he said. "That makes it easier and cheaper besides."

She confessed to me that he'd managed to impress her, but for reasons opposite those of love. "I detested conceited men, and I'd never seen one so stuck-up," she told me, recalling that day. "Besides, I thought he was a Jew." Her annoyance was greater when she sang out the raffle number for the music box, to the anxiety of all, and indeed, it had been won by Bayardo San Román. She couldn't imagine that he, just to impress her, had bought all the tickets in the raffle.

That night, when she returned home, Angela Vicario found the music box there, gift-wrapped and tied with an organdy bow. "I never did find out how he knew that it was my birthday," she told me. It was hard for her to convince her parents that she hadn't given Bayardo San Román any reason to send her a gift like that, and even worse, in such a visible way that it hadn't gone unnoticed by anyone. So her older brothers, Pedro and Pablo, took the music box to the hotel to give back to its owner, and they did it with such a rush that there was no one to witness them come and then not leave. Since the only thing the family hadn't counted upon was Bayardo San Román's irresistible charm, the twins didn't reappear until dawn of the next day, foggy with drink, bearing once more the music box, and bringing along, besides, Bayardo San Román to continue the revels at home.

Angela Vicario was the youngest daughter of a family of scant resources. Her father, Poncio Vicario, was a poor man's goldsmith, and he'd lost his sight from doing so much fine work in gold in order to maintain the honor of the house. Purísima del Carmen, her mother, had been a schoolteacher until she married for ever. Her meek and somewhat afflicted look hid the strength of her character quite well. "She looked like a nun," my wife Mercedes recalls. She devoted herself with such spirit of sacrifice to the care of her husband and the rearing of her children that at times one forgot she still existed. The two oldest daughters had married very late. In addition to the twins, there was a middle daughter who had died of nighttime fevers, and two years later they were still observing a mourning that was relaxed inside the house but rigorous on the street. The brothers were brought up to be men. The girls had been reared to get married. They knew how to do screen embroidery, sew by machine, weave bone lace, wash and iron, make artificial flowers and fancy candy, and write engagement announcements. Unlike other girls of the time, who had neglected the cult of death, the four were past mistresses in the ancient science of sitting up with the ill, comforting the dying, and enshrouding the dead. The only thing that my mother reproached them for was the custom of combing their hair before sleeping. "Girls," she would tell them, "don't comb your hair at night; you'll slow down seafarers." Except for that, she thought there were no better-reared daughters. "They're perfect," she was frequently heard to say. "Any man will be happy with them because they've been raised to suffer." Yet it was difficult for the men who married the two eldest to break the circle, because they always went together everywhere, and they organized dances for women only and were predisposed to find hidden intentions in the designs of men.

Angela Vicario was the prettiest of the four, and my mother said that she had been born like the great queens of history, with the umbilical cord wrapped around her neck. But she had a helpless air and a poverty of spirit that augured an uncertain future for her. I would see her again year after year during my Christmas vacations, and every time she seemed more destitute in the window of her house, where she would sit in the afternoon making cloth flowers and singing songs about single women with her neighbors. "She's all set to be hooked," Santiago Nasar would tell me, "your cousin the ninny is." Suddenly, a little before the mourning for her sister, I passed her on the street for the first time dressed as a grown woman and with her hair curled, and I could scarcely believe it was the same person. But it was a momentary vision: her penury of spirit had been aggravated with the years. So much so that when it was discovered that Bayardo San Román wanted to marry her, many people thought it was an outsider's scheming.

The family took it not only seriously but with great excitement. Except Pura Vicario, who laid down the condition that Bayardo San Román should identify himself properly. Up till then nobody knew who he was. His past didn't go beyond that afternoon when he disembarked in his actor's getup, and he was so reserved about his origins that even the most demented invention could have been true. It came to be said that he had wiped out villages and sown terror in Casanare as troop commander, that he had escaped from Devil's Island, that he'd been seen in Pernambuco trying to make a living with a pair of trained bears, and that he'd salvaged the remains of a Spanish galleon loaded with gold in the Windward Passage. Bayardo San Román put an end to all those conjectures by a simple recourse: he produced his entire family.

There were four of them: the father, the mother, and two provocative sisters. They arrived in a Model T Ford with official plates, whose duck-quack horn aroused the streets at eleven o'clock in the morning. His mother, Alberta Simonds, a big mulatto woman from Curaçao, who spoke Spanish with a mixture of Papiamento, in her youth had been proclaimed the most beautiful of the two hundred most beautiful women in the Antilles. The sisters, newly come into bloom, were like two restless fillies. But the main attraction was the father: General Petronio San Román, hero of the civil wars of the past century, and one of the major glories of the Conservative regime for having put Colonel Aureliano Buendía to flight in the disaster of Tucurinca. My mother was the only one who wouldn't go to greet him when she found out who he was. "It seems all right to me that they should get married," she told me. "But that's one thing and it's something altogether different to shake hands with the man who gave the orders for Gerineldo Márquez to be shot in the back." As soon as he appeared in the window of the automobile waving his white hat, everybody recognized him because of the fame of his pictures. He was wearing a wheat-colored linen suit, high-laced cordovan shoes, and gold-rimmed glasses held by a clasp on the bridge of his nose and connected by a chain to a buttonhole in his vest. He wore the Medal of Valor on his lapel and carried a cane with the national shield carved on the pommel. He was the first to get out of the automobile, completely covered with the burning dust of our bad roads, and all he had to do was appear on the running board for everyone to realize that Bayardo San Román was going to marry whomever he chose.

It was Angela Vicario who didn't want to marry him. "He seemed too much of a man for me," she told me. Besides, Bayardo San Román hadn't even tried to court her, but had bewitched the family with his charm. Angela Vicario never forgot the horror of the night on which her parents and her older sisters with their husbands, gathered together in the parlor, imposed on her the obligation to marry a man whom she had barely seen. The twins stayed out of it. "It looked to us like woman problems," Pablo Vicario told me. The parents' decisive argument was that a family dignified by modest means had no right to disdain that prize of destiny. Angela Vicario only dared hint at the inconvenience of a lack of love, but her mother demolished it with a single phrase:

"Love can be learned too."

Unlike engagements of the time, which were long and supervised, theirs lasted only four months due to Bayardo San Román's urgings. It wasn't any shorter because Pura Vicario demanded that they wait until the family mourning was over. But the time passed without anxiety because of the irresistible way in which Bayardo San Román arranged things. "One night he asked me what house I liked best," Angela Vicario told me. "And I answered, without knowing why, that the prettiest house in town was the farmhouse belonging to the widower Xius." I would have said the same. It was on a windswept hill, and from the terrace you could see the limitless paradise of the marshes covered with purple anemones, and on clear summer days you could make out the neat horizon of the Caribbean and the tourist ships from Cartagena de Indias. That very night Bayardo San Román went to the social club and sat down at the widower Xius's table to play a game of dominoes.

"Widower," he told him, "I'll buy your house."

"It's not for sale," the widower said.

"I'll buy it along with everything inside."

The widower Xius explained to him with the good breeding of olden days that the objects in the house had been bought by his wife over a whole lifetime of sacrifice and that for him they were still a part of her. "He was speaking with his heart in his hand," I was told by Dr. Dionisio Iguarán, who was playing with them. "I was sure he would have died before he'd sell a house where he'd been happy for over thirty years." Bayardo San Román also understood his reasons.

"Agreed," he said. "So sell me the house empty."

But the widower defended himself until the

end of the game. Three nights later, better prepared, Bayardo San Román returned to the domino table.

"Widower," he began again, "what's the price of the house?"

"It hasn't got a price."

"Name any one you want."

"I'm sorry, Bayardo," the widower said, "but you young people don't understand the motives of the heart."

Bayardo San Román didn't pause to think.

"Let's say five thousand pesos," he said.

"You don't beat around the bush," the widower answered him, his dignity aroused. "The house isn't worth all that."

"Ten thousand," said Bayardo San Román. "Right now and with one bill on top of another."

The widower looked at him, his eyes full of tears. "He was weeping with rage," I was told by Dr. Dionisio Iguarán, who, in addition to being a physician, was a man of letters. "Just imagine: an amount like that within reach and having to say no from a simple weakness of the spirit." The widower Xius's voice didn't come out, but without hesitation he said no with his head.

"Then do me one last favor," said Baynardo

San Román. "Wait for me here for five minutes."

Five minutes later, indeed, he returned to the social club with his silver-trimmed saddlebags, and on the table he laid ten bundles of thousand-peso notes with the printed bands of the State Bank still on them. The widower Xius died two months later. "He died because of that," Dr. Dionisio Iguarán said. "He was healthier than the rest of us, but when you listened with the stethoscope you could hear the tears bubbling inside his heart." But not only had he sold the house with everything in it; he asked Bayard San Román to pay him little by little because he didn't even have an old trunk where he could keep so much consolation money.

No one would have thought, nor did anyone say, that Angela Vicario wasn't a virgin. She hadn't known any previous fiancé and she'd grown up along with her sisters under the rigor of a mother of iron. Even when it was less than two months before she would be married, Pura Vicario wouldn't let her go out alone with Bayardo San Román to see the house where they were going to live, but she and the blind father accompanied her to watch over her honor. "The only thing I prayed to God for was to give me the courage to kill myself," Angela Vicario told me. "But he didn't give it to me." She was so distressed that she had resolved to tell her mother the truth so as to free herself from that martyrdom, when her only two confidantes, who worked with her making cloth flowers, dissuaded her from her good intentions. "I obeyed them blindly," she told me, "because they made me believe that they were experts in men's tricks." They assured her that almost all women lost their virginity in childhood accidents. They insisted that even the most difficult of husbands resigned themselves to anything as long as nobody knew about it. They convinced her, finally, that most men came to their wedding night so frightened that they were incapable of doing anything without the woman's help, and at the moment of truth they couldn't answer for their own acts. "The only thing they believe is what they see on the sheet," they told her. And they taught her old wives' tricks to feign her lost possession, so that on her first morning as a newlywed she could display open under the sun in the courtyard of her house the linen sheet with the stain of honor.

She got married with that illusion. Bayardo San Román, for his part, must have got married with the illusion of buying happiness with the huge weight of his power and fortune, for the more the plans for the festival grew, the more delirious ideas occurred to him to make it even larger. He tried to hold off the wedding for a day when the bishop's visit was announced so that he could marry them, but Angela Vicario was against it. "Actually," she told me, "the fact is I didn't want to be blessed by a man who cut off only the combs for soup and threw the rest of the rooster into the garbage." Yet, even without the bishop's blessing, the festival took on a force of its own so difficult to control that it got out of the hands of Bayardo San Román and ended up being a public event.

General Petronio San Román and his family arrived that time on the National Congress's ceremonial boat, which remained moored to the dock until the end of the festivities, and with them came many illustrious people who, even so, passed unnoticed in the tumult of new faces. So many gifts were brought that it was necessary to restore the forgotten site of the first electrical power plant in order to display the most valuable among them, and the rest were immediately taken to the former home of the widower Xius, which had already been prepared to receive the newlyweds. The groom received a convertible with his name engraved in Gothic letters under the manufacturer's seal. The bride was given a chest with table settings in pure gold for twenty-four guests. They also brought in a ballet company and two waltz orchestras that played out of tune with the local bands and all the groups of brass and accordion players who came, animated by the uproar of the revelry.

The Vicario family lived in a modest house with brick walls and a palm roof, topped by two attics where in January swallows got in to breed. In front it had a terrace almost completely covered with flowerpots, and a large yard with hens running loose and with fruit trees. In the rear of the yard the twins had a pigsty, with its sacrificial stone and its disemboweling table, which had been a good source of domestic income ever since Poncio Vicario had lost his sight. Pedro Vicario had started the business, but when he went into military service, his twin brother also learned the slaughterer's trade.

The inside of the house barely had enough room in which to live, and so the older sisters tried to borrow a house when they realized the size of the festival. "Just imagine," Angela Vicario told me, "they'd thought about Plácida Linero's house, but luckily my parents stubbornly held to the old song that our daughters would be married in our pigpen or they wouldn't be married at all." So they painted the house its original yellow color, fixed up the doors, repaired the floors, and left it as worthy as was possible for such a clamorous wedding. The twins took the pigs off elsewhere and sanitized the pigsty with quicklime, but even so it was obvious that there wasn't enough room. Finally, through the efforts of Bayardo San Román, they knocked down the fences in the yard, borrowed the neighboring house for dancing, and set up carpenters' benches to sit and eat on under the leaves of the tamarind trees.

The only unforeseen surprise was caused by the groom on the morning of the wedding, for he was two hours late in coming for Angela Vicario and she had refused to get dressed as a bride until she saw him in the house. "Just imagine," she told me. "I would have been happy even if he hadn't come, but never if he abandoned me dressed up." Her caution seemed natural, because there was no public misfortune more shameful than for a woman to be jilted in her bridal gown. On the other hand, the fact that Angela Vicario dared put on the veil and the orange blossoms without being a virgin would be interpreted afterwards as a profanation of the symbols of purity. My mother was the only one who appreciated as an act of courage the fact that she had played out her marked cards to the final consequences. "In those days," she explained to me, "God understood such things." But no one yet knew what cards Bayardo San Román was playing. From the moment he finally appeared in frock coat and top hat until he fled the dance with the creature of his torment, he was the perfect image of a happy bridegroom.

Nor was it known what cards Santiago Nasar was playing. I was with him all the time, in the church and at the festival, along with Cristo Bedoya and my brother Luis Enrique, and none of us caught a glimpse of any change in his manner. I've had to repeat this many times, because the four of us had grown up together in school and later on in the same gang at vacation time, and nobody could have believed that one of us could have a secret without its being shared, particularly such a big secret.

Santiago Nasar was a man for parties, and he had his best time on the eve of his death calculating the expense of the wedding. He estimated that they'd set up floral decorations in the church equal in cost to those for fourteen first-class funerals. That precision would haunt me for many years, because Santiago Nasar had often told me that the smell of closed-in flowers had an immediate relation to death for him, and that day he repeated it to me as we went into the church. "I don't want any flowers at my funeral," he told me, hardly thinking that I would see to it that there weren't any the next day. En route from the church to the Vicarios' house he drew up the figures for the colored wreaths that decorated the streets, calculated the cost of the music and the rockets, and even the hail of raw rice with which they received us at the party. In the drowsiness of noon, the newlyweds made their rounds in the yard. Bayardo San Román had become our very good friend, a friend of a few drinks, as they said in those days, and he seemed very much at ease at our table. Angela Vicario, without her veil and bridal bouquet and in her sweat-stained satin dress, had suddenly taken on the face of a married woman. Santiago Nasar calculated, and told Bayardo San Román, that up to then the wedding was costing some nine thousand pesos. It was obvious that Angela took this as an impertinence. "My mother taught me never to talk about money in front of other people," she told me. Bayardo San Román, on the other hand, took it very graciously and even with a certain pride.

"Almost," he said, "but we're only beginning. When it's all over it will be twice that, more or less."

Santiago Nasar proposed proving it down to the last penny, and his life lasted just long enough. In fact, with the final figures that Cristo Bedoya gave him the next day on the docks, forty-five minutes before he died, he ascertained that Bayardo San Román's prediction had been exact.

I had a very confused memory of the festival before I decided to rescue it piece by piece from the memory of others. For years they went on talking in my house about the fact that my father had gone back to playing his boyhood violin in honor of the newlyweds, that my sister the nun had danced a merengue in her doorkeeper's habit, and that Dr. Dionisio Iguarán, who was my mother's cousin, had arranged for them to take him off on the official boat so he wouldn't be here the next day when the bishop arrived. In the course of the investigations for this chronicle I recovered numerous marginal experiences, among them the free recollections of Bayardo San Román's sisters, whose velvet dresses with great butterfly wings pinned to their backs with gold brooches drew more attention than the plumed hat and row of war medals worn by their father. Many knew that in the confusion of the bash I had proposed marriage to Mercedes Barcha as soon as she finished primary school, just as she herself would remind me fourteen years later when we got married. Really, the most intense image that I have always held of that unwelcome Sunday was that of old Poncio Vicario sitting alone on a stool in the center of the yard. They had placed him there thinking perhaps that it was the seat of honor, and the guests stumbled over him, confused him with someone else, moved him so he wouldn't be in the way, and he nodded his snow-white head in all directions with the erratic expression of someone too recently blind, answering questions that weren't directed at him and responding to fleeting waves of the hand that no one was making to him, happy in his circle of oblivion, his shirt cardboard-stiff with starch and holding the lignum vitae cane they had bought him for the party.

The formal activities ended at six in the afternoon, when the guests of honor took their leave. The boat departed with all its lights burning, and with a wake of waltzes from the player piano, and for an instant we were cast adrift over an abyss of uncertainty, until we recognized each other again and plunged into the confusion of the bash. The newlyweds appeared a short time later in the open car, making their way with difficulty through the tumult. Bayardo San Román shot off rockets, drank cane liquor from the bottles the crowd held out to him, and got out of the car with Angela Vicario to join the whirl of the *cumbiamba* dance. Finally, he ordered us to keep on dancing at his expense for as long as our lives would reach, and he carried his terrified wife off to his dream house, where the widower Xius had been happy.

The public spree broke up into fragments at around midnight, and all that remained was Clotilde Armenta's establishment on one side of the square. Santiago Nasar and I, with my brother Luis Enrique and Cristo Bedoya, went to María Alejandrina Cervantes's house of mercies. Among so many others, the Vicario brothers were there and they were drinking with us and singing with Santiago Nasar five hours before killing him. A few scattered embers from the original party must still have remained, because from all sides waves of music and distant fights reached us, sadder and sadder, until a short while before the bishop's boat bellowed.

Pura Vicario told my mother that she had gone to bed at eleven o'clock at night after her older daughters had helped her clean up a bit from the devastation of the wedding. Around ten o'clock, when there were still a few drunkards singing in the square, Angela Vicario had sent for a little suitcase of personal things that were in the dresser in her bedroom, and she asked them also to send a suitcase with everyday clothes; the messenger was in a hurry. Pura Vicario had fallen into a deep sleep, when there was knocking on the door. "They were three very slow knocks," she told my mother, "but they had that strange touch of bad news about them." She told her that she'd opened the door without turning on the light so as not to awaken anybody and saw Bayardo San Román in the glow of the street light, his silk shirt unbuttoned and his fancy pants held up by elastic suspenders. "He had that green color of dreams," Pura Vicario told my mother. Angela Vicario was in the shadows, so she saw only her when Bayardo San Román grabbed her by the arm and brought her into the light. Her satin dress was in shreds and she was wrapped in a towel up to the waist. Pura Vicario thought they'd gone off the road in the car and were lying dead at the bottom of the ravine.

"Holy Mother of God," she said in terror. "Answer me if you're still of this world."

Bayardo San Román didn't enter, but softly pushed his wife into the house without speaking a word. Then he kissed Pura Vicario on the cheek and spoke to her in a very deep, dejected voice, but with great tenderness. "Thank you for everything, Mother," he told her. "You're a saint."

Only Pura Vicario knew what she did during the next two hours, and she went to her grave with her secret. "The only thing I can remember is that she was holding me by the hair with one hand and beating me with the other with such rage that I thought she was going to kill me," Angela Vicario told me. But even that she did with such stealth that her husband and her older daughters, asleep in the other rooms, didn't find out about anything until dawn, when the disaster had already been consummated.

The twins returned home a short time before three, urgently summoned by their mother. They found Angela Vicario lying face down on the dining room couch, her face all bruised, but she'd stopped crying. "I was no longer frightened," she told me. "On the contrary: I felt as if the drowsiness of death had finally been lifted from me, and the only thing I wanted was for it all to be over quickly so I could flop down and go to sleep." Pedro Vicario, the more forceful of the brothers, picked her up by the waist and sat her on the dining room table.

"All right, girl," he said to her, trembling with rage, "tell us who it was."

She only took the time necessary to say the name. She looked for it in the shadows, she found it at first sight among the many, many easily confused names from this world and the other, and she nailed it to the wall with her well-aimed dart, like a butterfly with no will whose sentence has always been written.

"Santiago Nasar," she said.

THE LAWYER STOOD BY THE THESIS OF homicide in legitimate defense of honor, which was upheld by the court in good faith, and the twins declared at the end of the trial that they would have done it again a thousand times over for the same reason. It was they who gave a hint of the direction the defense would take as soon as they surrendered to their church a few minutes after the crime. They burst panting into the parish house, closely pursued by a group of roused-up Arabs, and they laid the knives, with clean blades, on Father Amador's desk. Both were exhausted from the barbarous work of death, and their clothes and arms were soaked and their faces smeared with sweat and still living blood, but the priest recalled the surrender as an act of great dignity.

"We killed him openly," Pedro Vicario said, "but we're innocent."

"Perhaps before God," said Father Amador.

"Before God and before men," Pablo Vicario said. "It was a matter of honor."

Furthermore, with the reconstruction of the facts, they had feigned a much more unforgiving bloodthirstiness than really was true, to such an extreme that it was necessary to use public funds to repair the main door of Plaćida Linero's house, which was all chipped with knife thrusts. In the panopticon of Riohacha, where they spent three years awaiting trial because they couldn't afford bail, the older prisoners remembered them for their good character and sociability, but they never noticed any indication of remorse in them. Still, in reality it seemed that the Vicario brothers had done nothing right with a view to killing Santiago Nasar immediately and without any public spectacle, but had done much more than could be imagined to have someone to stop them from killing him, and they had failed.

According to what they told me years later, they had begun by looking for him at María Alejandrina Cervantes's place, where they had been with him until two o'clock. That fact, like many others, was not reported in the brief. Actually, Santiago Nasar was no longer there at the time the twins said they went looking for him, because we'd left on a round of serenades, but in any case, it wasn't certain that they'd gone. "They never would have left here," Maria Alejandrina Cervantes told me, and knowing her so well, I never doubted it. On the other hand, they did go to wait for him at Clotilde Armenta's place, where they knew that almost everybody would turn up except Santiago Nasar. "It was the only place open," they declared to the investigator. "Sooner or later he would have to come out," they told me, after they had been absolved. Still, everybody knew that the main door of Plácida Linero's house was always barred on the inside, even during the daytime, and that Santiago Nasar always carried the keys to the back door with him. That was where he went in when he got home, in fact, while the Vicario twins had been waiting for him for more than an hour on the other side, and if he later left by the door on the square when he went to receive the bishop, it was for such an unforeseen reason that the investigator who drew up the brief never did understand it.

There had never been a death more foretold. After their sister revealed the name to them, the Vicario twins went to the bin in the pigsty where they kept their sacrificial tools and picked out the two best knives: one for quartering, ten inches long by two and a half inches wide, and the other for trimming, seven inches long by one and a half inches wide. They wrapped them in a rag and went to sharpen them at the meat market, where only a few stalls had begun to open. There weren't very many customers that early, but twenty-two people declared they had heard everything said, and they all coincided in the impression that the only reason the brothers had said it was so that someone would come over to hear them. Faustino Santos, a butcher friend, saw them enter at three-twenty, when he had just opened up his innards table, and he couldn't

understand why they were coming on a Monday and so early, and still in their dark wedding suits. He was accustomed to seeing them on Fridays, but a little later, and wearing the leather aprons they put on for slaughtering. "I thought they were so drunk," Faustino Santos told me, "that not only had they forgotten what time it was, but what day it was too." He reminded them that it was Monday.

"Everybody knows that, you dope," Pablo Vicario answered him good-naturedly. "We just came to sharpen our knives."

They sharpened them on the grindstone, and the way they always did: Pedro holding the knives and turning them over on the stone, and Pablo working the crank. At the same time, they talked with the other butchers about the splendor of the wedding. Some of them complained about not having gotten their share of cake, in spite of their being working companions, and they promised them to have some sent over later. Finally, they made the knives sing on the stone, and Pablo laid his beside the lamp so that the steel sparkled.

"We're going to kill Santiago Nasar," he said.

Their reputation as good people was so well-founded that no one paid any attention to them. "We thought it was drunkards' baloney," several butchers declared, just as Victoria Guzmán and so many others did who saw them later. I was to ask the butchers sometime later whether or not the trade of slaughterer didn't reveal a soul predisposed to killing a human being. They protested: "When you sacrifice a steer you don't dare look into its eyes." One of them told me that he couldn't eat the flesh of an animal he had butchered. Another said that he wouldn't be capable of sacrificing a cow if he'd known it before, much less if he'd drunk its milk. I reminded them that the Vicario brothers sacrificed the same hogs they raised, which were so familiar to them that they called them by their names. "That's true," one of them replied, "but remember that they didn't give them people's names but the names of flowers." Faustino Santos was the only one who perceived a glimmer of truth in Pablo Vicario's threat, and he asked him jokingly why they had to kill Santiago Nasar since there were so many other rich people who deserved dying first.

"Santiago Nasar knows why," Pedro Vicario answered him.

Faustino Santos told me that he'd still been doubtful, and that he reported it to a policeman who came by a little later to buy a pound of liver for the mayor's breakfast. The policeman, according to the brief, was named Leandro Pornoy, and he died the following year, gored in the jugular vein by a bull during the national holidays, so I was never able to talk to him. But Clotilde Armenta confirmed for me that he was the first person in her store when the Vicario twins were sitting and waiting there.

Clotilde Armenta had just replaced her husband behind the counter. It was their usual system. The shop sold milk at dawn and provisions during the day and became a bar after six o'clock in the evening. Clotilde Armenta would open at three-thirty in the morning. Her husband, the good Don Rogelio de la Flor, would take charge of the bar until closing time. But that night there had been so many stray customers from the wedding that he went to bed after three o'clock without closing, and Clotilde Armenta was already up earlier than usual because she wanted to finish before the bishop arrived.

The Vicario brothers came in at four-ten. At that time only things to eat were sold, but Clotilde Armenta sold them a bottle of cane liquor, not only because of the high regard she had for them but also because she was very grateful for the piece of wedding cake they had sent her. They drank down the whole bottle in two long swigs, but they remained stolid. "They were stunned," Clotilde Armenta told me, "and they couldn't have got their blood pressure up even with lamp oil." Then they took off their cloth jackets, hung them carefully on the chair backs, and asked her for another bottle. Their shirts were dirty with dried sweat and a one-day beard gave them a backwoods look. They drank the second bottle more slowly, sitting down, looking insistently toward Plácida Linero's house on the sidewalk across the way, where the windows were dark. The largest one, on the balcony, belonged to Santiago Nasar's bedroom. Pedro Vicario asked Clotilde Armenta if she had seen any light in that window, and she answered him no, but it seemed like a strange thing to be interested in.

"Did something happen to him?" she asked.

"No," Pedro Vicario replied. "Just that we're looking for him to kill him."

It was such a spontaneous answer that she couldn't believe she'd heard right. But she noticed that the twins were carrying two butcher knives wrapped in kitchen rags.

"And might a person know why you want to

kill him so early in the morning?" she asked.

"He knows why," Pedro Vicario answered.

Clotilde Armenta examined them seriously: she knew them so well that she could tell them apart, especially ever since Pedro Vicario had come back from the army. "They looked like two children," she told me. And that thought frightened her, because she'd always felt that only children are capable of everything. So she finished getting the jug of milk ready and went to wake her husband to tell him what was going on in the shop. Don Rogelio de la Flor listened to her half-awake.

"Don't be silly," he said to her. "Those two aren't about to kill anybody, much less someone rich."

When Clotilde Armenta returned to the store, the twins were chatting with Officer Leandro Pornoy, who was coming for the mayor's milk. She didn't hear what they were talking about, but she supposed that they had told him something about their plans from the way he looked at the knives when he left.

Colonel Lázaro Aponte had just got up a little before four. He'd finished shaving when Officer Leandro Pornoy revealed the Vicario brothers' intentions to him. He'd settled so many fights between friends the night before that he was in no hurry for another one. He got dressed calmly, tied his bow tie several times until he had it perfect, and around his neck he hung the scapular of the Congregation of Mary, to receive the bishop. While he breakfasted on fried liver smothered with onion rings, his wife told him with great excitement that Bayardo San Román had brought Angela Vicario back home, but he didn't take it dramatically.

"Good Lord!" he mocked. "What will the bishop think!"

Nevertheless, before finishing breakfast he remembered what the orderly had just told him, put the two bits of news together, and discovered immediately that they fit like pieces of a puzzle. Then he went to the square, going along the street to the new dock, where the houses were beginning to liven up for the bishop's arrival. "I can remember with certainty that it was almost five o'clock and it was beginning to rain," Colonel Lázaro Aponte told me. Along the way three people stopped him to inform him in secret that the Vicario brothers were waiting for Santiago Nasar to kill him, but only one person could tell him where.

He found them in Clotilde Armenta's store. "When I saw them I thought they were nothing but a pair of big bluffers," he told me with his personal logic, "because they weren't as drunk as I thought." Nor did he interrogate them concerning their intentions, but took away their knives and sent them off to sleep. He treated them with the same self-assurance with which he had passed off his wife's alarm.

"Just imagine!" he told them. "What will the bishop say if he finds you in that state!"

They left. Clotilde Armenta suffered another disappointment with the mayor's casual attitude, because she thought he should have detained the twins until the truth came out. Colonel Aponte showed her the knives as a final argument.

"Now they haven't got anything to kill anybody with," he said.

"That's not why," said Clotilde Armenta. "It's to spare those poor boys from the horrible duty that's fallen on them."

Because she'd sensed it. She was certain that the Vicario brothers were not as eager to carry out the sentence as to find someone who would do them the favor of stopping them. But Colonel Aponte was at peace with his soul.

"No one is arrested just on suspicion," he said. "Now it's a matter of warning Santiago Nasar, and happy new year."

Clotilde Armenta would always remember that Colonel Aponte's chubby appearance evoked a certain pity in her, but on the other hand I remembered him as a happy man, although a little bit off due to the solitary spiritualist practices he had learned through the mails. His behavior that Monday was the final proof of his silliness. The truth is that he didn't think of Santiago Nasar again until he saw him on the docks, and then he congratulated himself for having made the right decision.

The Vicario brothers had told their plans to more than a dozen people who had gone to buy milk, and these had spread the news everywhere before six o'clock. It seemed impossible to Clotilde Armenta that they didn't know in the house across the way. She didn't think that Santiago Nasar was there, since she hadn't seen the bedroom light go on, and she asked all the people she could to warn him when they saw him. She even sent word to Father Amador through the novice on duty, who came to buy milk for the nuns. After four o'clock, when she saw the lights in the kitchen of Plácida Linero's house, she sent the last urgent message to Victoria Guzmán by the beggar woman who came every day to ask for a little milk in the name of charity. When the bishop's boat bellowed, almost everybody was up to receive him and there were very few of us who didn't know that the Vicario twins were waiting for Santiago Nasar to kill him, and, in addition, the reasons were understood down to the smallest detail.

Clotilde Armenta hadn't finished dispensing her milk when the Vicario brothers returned with two other knives wrapped up in newspapers. One was for quartering, with a strong, rusty blade twelve inches long and three inches wide, which had been put together by Pedro Vicario with the metal from a marquetry saw at a time when German knives were no longer available because of the war. The other one was shorter, but broad and curved. The investigator had made sketches of them in the brief, perhaps because he had trouble describing them, and all he ventured to say was that this one looked like a miniature scimitar. It was with these knives that the crime was committed, and both were rudimentary and had seen a lot of use.

Faustino Santos couldn't understand what had happened. "They came to sharpen their knives a second time," he told me, "and once more they shouted for people to hear that they were going to cut Santiago Nasar's guts out, so I believed they were kidding around, especially since I didn't pay any attention to the knives and thought they were the same ones." This time, however, Clotilde Armenta noticed from the moment she saw them enter that they didn't have the same determination as before.

Actually, they'd had their first disagreement. Not only were they much more different inside than they looked on the outside, but in difficult emergencies they showed opposite characters. We, their friends, had spotted it ever since grammar school. Pablo Vicario was six minutes older than his brother, and he was the more imaginative and resolute until adolescence. Pedro Vicario always seemed more sentimental to me, and by the same token more authoritarian. They presented themselves together for military service at the age of twenty, and Pablo Vicario was excused in order to stay home and take care of the family. Pedro Vicario served for eleven months on police patrol. The army routine, aggravated by the fear of death, had matured his tendency to command and the habit of deciding for his brother. He also came back with a case of sergeant's blennorrhea that resisted the most brutal methods of military medicine as well as the arsenic injections and permanganate purges of Dr. Dionisio Iguarán. Only in jail did they manage to cure it. We, his friends, agreed that Pablo Vicario had suddenly developed the strange dependence of a younger brother when Pedro Vicario returned with a barrack-room soul and with the novel trick of lifting his shirt for anyone who wanted to see a bullet wound with seton on his left side. He even began to develop a kind of fervor over the great man's blennorrhea that his brother wore like a war medal.

Pedro Vicario, according to his own declaration, was the one who made the decision to kill Santiago Nasar, and at first his brother only followed along. But he was also the one who considered his duty fulfilled when the mayor disarmed them, and then it was Pablo Vicario who assumed command. Neither of the two mentioned that disagreement in their separate statements to the investigator, but Pablo Vicario confirmed several times to me that it hadn't been easy for him to convince his brother of their final resolve. Maybe it was really nothing but a wave of panic, but the fact is that Pablo Vicario went into the pigsty alone to get the other two knives, while his brother agonized, drop by drop, trying to urinate under the tamarind trees. "My brother never knew what it was like," Pedro Vicario told me in our only interview. "It was like pissing ground glass." Pablo Vicario found him hugging the tree when he came back with the knives. "He was in a cold sweat from the pain," he said to me, "and he tried to tell me to go on by myself because he was in no condition to kill anybody." He sat down on one of the carpenters' benches they'd set up under the trees for the wedding lunch, and he dropped his pants down to his knees. "He spent about half an hour changing the gauze he had his prick wrapped in," Pablo Vicario told me. Actually, he hadn't delayed more than ten minutes, but this was something so difficult and so puzzling for Pablo Vicario that he interpreted it as some new trick on his brother's part to waste time until dawn. So he put the knife in his hand and dragged him off almost by force in search of their sister's lost honor.

"There's no way out of this," he told him. "It's as if it had already happened."

They left by way of the pigpen gate with the knives unwrapped, trailed by the uproar of the dogs in the yards. It was beginning to get light. "It wasn't raining," Pablo Vicario remembered.

"Just the opposite," Pedro recalled. "There was a sea wind and you could still count the stars with your finger." The news had been so well spread by then that Hortensia Baute opened her door precisely as they were passing her house, and she was the first to weep for Santiago Nasar. "I thought they'd already killed him," she told me, "because I saw the knives in the light from the street lamp and it looked to me like they were dripping blood." One of the few houses open on that misbegotten street was that of Prudencia Cotes, Pablo Vicario's fiancée. Whenever the twins passed by there at that time, and especially on Fridays when they were going to the market, they would drop in to have their first cup of coffee. They pushed open the door to the courtyard, surrounded by the dogs, who recognized them in the half light of dawn, and they greeted Prudencia Cotes's mother in the kitchen. Coffee wasn't ready yet.

"We'll leave it for later," Pablo Vicario said. "We're in a hurry now."

"I can imagine, my sons," she said. "Honor doesn't wait."

But in any case, they waited, and this time it was Pedro Vicario who thought his brother was wasting time on purpose. While they were drinking their coffee, Prudencia Cotes came into the kitchen in all her adolescent bloom, carrying a roll of old newspapers to revive the fire in the stove. "I knew what they were up to," she told me, "and I didn't only agree, I never would have married him if he hadn't done what a man should do." Before leaving the kitchen, Pablo Vicario took two sections of newspaper from her and gave them to his brother to wrap the knives in. Prudencia Cotes stood waiting in the kitchen until she saw them leave by the courtyard door, and she went on waiting for three years without a moment of discouragement until Pablo Vicario got out of jail and became her husband for life.

"Take good care of yourselves," she told them.

So Clotilde Armenta had good reason when it seemed to her that the twins weren't as resolute as before, and she served them a bottle of rotgut rum with the hope of getting them dead drunk. "That day," she told me, "I realized just how alone we women are in the world!" Pedro Vicario asked to borrow her husband's shaving implements, and she brought him the brush, the soap, the hanging mirror, and the safety razor with a new blade, but he shaved with his butcher knife. Clotilde Armenta thought that was the height of machismo. "He looked like a killer in the movies," she told me. But as he explained to me later, and it was true, in the army he'd learned to shave with a straight razor and couldn't do it any other way ever since. His brother, for his part, shaved in a more humble way, with Don Rogelio de la Flor's borrowed safety razor. Finally, they drank the bottle in silence, very slowly, gazing with the boobish look of early risers at the dark window in the house across the way, while fake customers buying milk they didn't need and asking for food items that didn't exist went in and out with the purpose of seeing whether it was true that they were waiting for Santiago Nasar to kill him.

The Vicario brothers would not see that window light up. Santiago Nasar went into the house at four-twenty, but he didn't have to turn on any light to reach his bedroom because the bulb on the stairway stayed lit through the night. He threw himself onto his bed in the darkness and with his clothes on, since he had only an hour in which to sleep, and that was how Victoria

Guzmán found him when she came up to wake him so he could receive the bishop. We'd been together at María Alejandrina Cervantes's until after three, when she herself sent the musicians away and turned out the lights in the dancing courtyard so that her pleasurable mulatto girls could go to bed by themselves and get some rest. They'd been working without cease for three days, first taking care of the guests of honor in secret, and then turned loose, the doors wide open for those of us still unsated by the wedding bash. María Alejandrina Cervantes, about whom we used to say that she would go to sleep only once and that would be to die, was the most elegant and the most tender woman I have ever known, and the most serviceable in bed, but she was also the strictest. She'd been born and reared here, and here she lived, in a house with open doors, with several rooms for rent and an enormous courtyard for dancing lit by lantern gourds bought in the Chinese bazaars of Paramaribo. It was she who did away with my generation's virginity. She taught us much more than we should have learned, but she taught us above all that there's no place in life sadder than an empty bed. Santiago Nasar lost his senses the first time he saw her. I warned him: "'*A falcon who chases a warlike crane can only hope for a life of pain.'"* But he didn't listen to me, dazzled by Maria Alejandrina Cervantes's illusory calls. She was his mad passion, his mistress of tears at the age of fifteen, until Ibrahim Nasar drove him out of the bed with a whip and shut him up for more than a year on The Divine Face. Ever since then they were still linked by a serious affection, but without the disorder of love, and she had so much respect for him that she never again went to bed with anyone if he was present. During those last vacations she would send us off early with the pretext that she was tired, but she left the door unbarred and with a lamp lighted in the hall so that I could come in secretly.

Santiago Nasar had an almost magical talent for disguises, and his favorite sport was to confuse the identities of the mulatto girls. He would rifle the wardrobe of some to disguise the others, so that they all ended up feeling different from themselves and like the ones they weren't. On a certain occasion, one of them found herself repeated in another with such exactness that she had an attack of tears. "I felt like I'd stepped out of the mirror," she said. But that night María Alejandrina Cervantes wouldn't let Santiago Nasar indulge himself for the last time in his tricks as a transformer, and she prevented it with such flimsy pretexts that the bad taste left by that memory changed his life. So we took the musicians with us for a round of serenades, and we continued the party on our own, while the Vicario twins were waiting for Santiago Nasar to kill him. It was he who got the idea, at almost four o'clock, to go up the widower Xius's hill and sing for the newlyweds.

Not only did we sing under the windows, but we set off rockets and fireworks in the gardens, yet we didn't perceive any sign of life inside the farmhouse. It didn't occur to us that there was no one there, especially because the new car was by the door with its top still folded down and with the satin ribbons and bouquets of wax orange blossoms they had hung on it during the festivities. My brother Luis Enrique, who played the guitar like a professional at that time, improvised a song with matrimonial double meanings in honor of the newlyweds. Until then it hadn't rained; on the contrary, the moon was high in the sky and the air was clear, and at the bottom of the precipice you could see the trickle of light from the Saint Elmo's fire in the cemetery. On the other side you could make out the groves of blue banana trees in the moonlight, the sad swamps, and the phosphorescent line of the Caribbean on the horizon. Santiago Nasar pointed to an intermittent light at sea and told us that it was the soul in torment of a slave ship that had sunk with a cargo of blacks from Senegal across from the main harbor mouth at Cartagena de Indias. It wasn't possible to think that his conscience was bothering him, although at that time he didn't know that the ephemeral married life of Angela Vicario had come to an end two hours before. Bayardo San Román had taken her to her parents' house on foot so that the noise of the motor wouldn't betray his misfortune in advance, and he was back there alone and with the lights out in the widower Xius's happy farmhouse.

When we went down the hill my brother invited us to have some breakfast of fried fish at one of the lunch stands in the market, but Santiago Nasar was against it because he wanted to get an hour's sleep before the bishop arrived. He went along the riverbank with Cristo Bedoya, passing the poor people's eating places that were beginning to light up by the old harbor, and before turning the corner he waved good-bye. It was the last time we saw him.

Cristo Bedoya, whom he had agreed to meet later on at the docks, took leave of him at the back door of his house. The dogs barked at him as usual when they heard him come in, but he calmed them down in the half light with the tinkling of his keys. Victoria Guzmán was keeping watch over the coffeepot on the stove when he passed by the kitchen on his way into the house.

"White man," she called to him, "coffee will be ready soon."

Santiago Nasar told her that he'd have some later, and he asked her to tell Divina Flor to wake him up at five-thirty and bring him a clean change of clothes, just like the ones he had on. An instant after he'd gone to bed, Victoria Guzmán got the message from Clotilde Armenta sent via the milk beggar. At five-thirty she followed his orders to wake him, but she didn't send Divina Flor and went up to the bedroom herself with the suit of pure linen, because she never missed a chance to keep her daughter away from the claws of the seigneur.

María Alejandrina Cervantes had left the door of her house unbarred. I took leave of my brother, crossed the veranda where the mulatto girls' cats were sleeping curled up among the tulips, and opened the bedroom door without knocking. The lights were out, but as soon as I went in I caught the smell of a warm woman and I saw the eyes of an insomniac leopard in the darkness, and then I didn't know anything else about myself until the bells began to ring.

On his way to our house, my brother went in to buy some cigarettes at Clotilde Armenta's store. He'd drunk so much that his memories of that encounter were always quite confused, but he never forgot the fatal drink that Pedro Vicario offered him. "It was liquid fire," he told me. Pablo Vicario, who had fallen asleep, awoke with a start when he heard him come in, and he showed him the knife.

"We're going to kill Santiago Nasar," he told him.

My brother doesn't remember it. "But even if I did remember, I wouldn't have believed it," he told me many times. "Who the fuck would ever think that the twins would kill anyone, much less with a pig knife!" Then they asked him where Santiago Nasar was, because they'd seen the two of them together, and my brother didn't remember his own answer either. But Clotilde Armenta and the Vicario brothers were so startled when they heard it that it was left established in the brief in separate declarations. According to them, my brother said: "Santiago Nasar is dead." Then he delivered an episcopal blessing, stumbled over the threshold, and staggered out. In the middle of the square he crossed paths with Father Amador, who was going to the dock in his vestments, followed by an acolyte ringing the bell and several helpers carrying the altar for the bishop's field mass. The Vicario brothers crossed themselves when they saw them pass.

Clotilde Armenta told me that they'd lost their last hopes when the priest passed by her place. "I thought he hadn't got my message," she said. Nonetheless, Father Amador confessed to me many years later, retired from the world in the gloomy Calafell Rest Home, that he had in fact received Clotilde Armenta's message and others more peremptory while he was getting ready to go the docks. "The truth is I didn't know what to do," he told me. "My first thought was that it wasn't any business of mine but something for the civil authorities, but then I made up my mind to say something in passing to Plácida Linero." Yet when he crossed the square, he'd forgotten completely. "You have to understand," he told me, "that the bishop was coming on that unfortunate day." At the moment of the crime he felt such despair and was so disgusted with himself that the only thing he could think of was to ring the fire alarm.

My brother Luis Enrique entered the house through the kitchen door, which my mother left unlocked so my father wouldn't hear us come in. He went to the bathroom before going to bed, but he fell asleep sitting on the toilet, and when my brother Jaime got up to go to school he found him stretched out face down on the tile floor and singing in his sleep. My sister the nun, who wasn't going to wait for the bishop because she had an eighty-proof hangover, couldn't get him to wake up. "It was striking five when I went to the bathroom," she told me. Later, when my sister Margot went in to bathe before going to the docks, she managed with great effort to drag him to his bedroom. From the other side of sleep he heard the first bellows of the bishop's boat without awakening. Then he fell into a deep sleep, worn out by his carousing, until my sister the nun rushed into the bedroom, trying to put her habit on as she ran, and woke him up with her mad cry:

"They've killed Santiago Nasar!"

THE DAMAGE FROM THE KNIVES WAS only a beginning for the unforgiving autopsy that Father Carmen Amador found himself obliged to perform in Dr. Dionisio Iguarán's absence. "It was as if we killed him all over again after he was dead," the aged priest told me in his retirement at Calafell. "But it was an order from the mayor, and orders from the barbarian, stupid as they might have been, had to be obeyed." It wasn't entirely proper. In the confusion of that absurd Monday, Colonel Aponte had had an urgent telegraphic conversation with the governor of the province, and the latter authorized him to take the preliminary steps while he sent an investigating magistrate. The mayor was a former troop commander with no experience in matters of law, and he was too conceited to ask anyone who knew where he should begin. The first thing that bothered him was the autopsy. Cristo Bedoya, who was a medical student, managed to get out of it because of his intimate friendship with Santiago Nasar. The mayor thought that the body could be kept under refrigeration until Dr. Dionisio Iguarán came back, but he couldn't find a human-sized freezer, and the only one in the market that would serve the purpose was out of order. The body had been exposed to public view in the center of the living room, lying on a narrow iron cot while they were building a rich man's coffin for it. They'd brought in fans from the bedrooms and some neighboring houses, but there were so many people anxious to see it that they had to push back the furniture and take down the bird cages and pots of ferns, and even then the heat was unbearable. In addition, the dogs, aroused by the smell of death, increased the uneasiness. They hadn't stopped howling since I went into the house, when Santiago Nasar

was still in his death throes in the kitchen and I found Divina Flor weeping in great howls and holding them off with a stick.

"Help me," she shouted to me. "What they want is to eat his guts."

We locked them up in the stable. Plácida Linero later ordered them taken to some place far off until after the funeral. But toward noon, no one knew how, they escaped from where they were and burst madly into the house. Plácida Linero, just once, lost her grip.

"Those shitty dogs!" she shouted. "Kill them!"

The order was carried out immediately and the house was silent again. Until then there hadn't been any concern at all for the state of the body. The face had remained intact, with the same expression it wore when he was singing, and Cristo Bedoya had put the intestines back in place and wrapped the body in linen strips. Nevertheless, in the afternoon a syrup-colored liquid began to flow from the wounds, drawing flies, and a purple blotch appeared on the upper lip and spread out very slowly, like the shadow of a cloud on water, up to the hairline. His face, which had always been easy-going, took on a hostile expression, and his mother covered it with a handkerchief. Colonel Aponte understood then that they couldn't wait any longer and he ordered Father Amador to perform the autopsy. "It would be worse digging him up a week later," he said. The priest had studied medicine and surgery at Salamanca, but had entered the seminary before he was graduated, and even the mayor knew that his autopsy would have no legal standing. Nevertheless, he made him carry out the order.

It was a massacre, performed at the public school with the help of the druggist, who took notes, and a first-year medical student who was here on vacation. They had only a few instruments for minor surgery available and the rest were craftsmen's tools. But despite the havoc wrought on the body, Father Amador's report seemed in order and the investigator incorporated it in the brief as a useful piece of evidence.

Seven of the many wounds were fatal. The liver was almost sliced in pieces by two deep cuts on the anterior side. He had four incisions in the stomach, one of them so deep that it went completely through, and destroyed, the pancreas. He had six other, lesser perforations in the transverse colon and multiple wounds in the small intestine. The only one he had in the back, at the level of the third lumbar vertebra, had perforated the right kidney. The abdominal cavity was filled with large clots of blood, and in the midst of the morass of gastric contents appeared a medal of gold that Santiago Nasar had swallowed at the age of four. The thoracic cavity showed two perforations: one in the second right rib space that affected the lung, and another quite close to the left armpit. He also had six minor wounds on his arms and hands, and two horizontal cuts: one on the right thigh and the other in the abdominal muscles. He had a deep stab in the right hand. The report says: "It looked like a stigma of the crucified Christ." The encephalic mass weighed sixty grams more than that of a normal Englishman, and Father Amador noted in the report that Santiago Nasar had a superior intelligence and a brilliant future. Nevertheless, in the final note he pointed out a hypertrophy of the liver that he attributed to a poorly cured case of hepatitis. "That is to say," he told me, "he had only a few years of life left to him in any case." Dr. Dionisio Iguarán, who in fact had treated Santiago Nasar for hepatitis at the age of twelve, recalled that autopsy with indignation. "Only a priest could be so dumb," he told me. "There was never any way to make him understand that we tropical people have larger livers than greenhorn Galician Spaniards." The report concluded that the cause of death had been a massive hemorrhage brought on by any one of the seven major wounds.

They gave us back a completely different body. Half of the cranium had been destroyed by the trepanation, and the lady-killer face that death had preserved ended up having lost its identity. Furthermore, the priest had pulled out the sliced-up intestines by the roots, but in the end he didn't know what to do with them, and he gave them an angry blessing and threw them into the garbage pail. The last onlookers ranged about the schoolhouse windows lost their curiosity, the helper fainted, and Colonel Lázaro Aponte, who had seen and caused so many repressive massacres, became a vegetarian as well as a spiritualist. The empty shell, stuffed with rags and quicklime and sewed up crudely with coarse twine and baling needles, was on the point of falling apart when we put it into the new coffin with its silk quilt lining. "I thought it would last longer that way," Father Amador told me. Just the opposite happened, and we had to bury him hurriedly at dawn because he was in such bad shape that it was already unbearable in the house.

A cloudy Tuesday was breaking through. I didn't have the courage to sleep at the end of that oppressive time, and I pushed on the door of María Alejandrina Cervantes's house in case she hadn't put up the bar. The gourd lamps were burning where they hung from the trees, and in the courtyard for dancing there were several wood fires with huge steaming pots where the mulatto girls were putting mourning dye onto their party clothes. I found María Alejandrina Cervantes awake as always at dawn, and completely naked as always when there weren't any strangers in the house. She was squatting like a Turkish houri on her queenly bed across from a Babylonic platter of things to eat: veal cutlets, a boiled chicken, a pork loin, and a garnishing of plantains and vegetables that would have served five people. Disproportionate eating was always the only way she could ever mourn and I'd never seen her do it with such grief. I lay down by her side with my clothes on, barely speaking, and mourning too in my way. I was thinking about the ferocity of Santiago Nasar's fate, which had collected twenty years of happiness from him not only with his death but also with the dismemberment of his body and its dispersion and extermination. I dreamed that a woman was coming into the room with a little girl in her arms, and that the child was chewing without stopping to take a breath, and that half-chewed kernels of corn were falling into the woman's brassiere. The woman said to me: "She crunches like a nutty nuthatch, kind of sloppy, kind of slurpy." Suddenly I felt the anxious fingers that were undoing the buttons of my shirt, and I caught the dangerous smell of the beast of love lying by my back, and I felt myself sinking into the delights of the quicksand of her tenderness. But suddenly she stopped, coughed from far off, and slipped out of my life.

"I can't," she said. "You smell of him."

Not just I. Everything continued smelling of Santiago Nasar that day. The Vicario brothers could smell him in the jail cell where the mayor had locked them up until he could think of something to do with them. "No matter how much I scrubbed with soap and rags, I couldn't get rid of the smell," Pedro Vicario told me. They'd gone three nights without sleep, but they couldn't rest because as soon as they began to fall asleep they would commit the crime all over again. Now, almost an old man, trying to explain to me his condition on that endless day, Pablo Vicario told me without any effort: "It was like being awake twice over." That phrase made me think that what must have been most unbearable for them in jail was their lucidity.

The room was ten feet square, and had a very high skylight with iron bars, a portable latrine, a washstand with its pitcher and basin, and two makeshift beds with straw mats. Colonel Aponte, under whose orders it had been built, said that no hotel existed that was more humane. My brother Luis Enrique agreed, because one night they'd locked him up after a fight among musicians, and the mayor allowed him the charity of having one of the mulatto girls stay with him. Perhaps the Vicario brothers could have thought the same thing at eight o'clock in the morning, when they felt themselves safe from the Arabs. At that moment they were comforted by the honor of having done their duty, and the only thing that worried them was the persistence of the smell. They asked for lots of water, laundry soap, and rags, and they washed the blood from their arms and faces, and they also washed their shirts, but they couldn't get any rest. Pedro Vicario asked for his laxatives and diuretics and a roll of sterile gauze so he could change his bandage, and he succeeded in having two urinations during the morning. Nevertheless, life was becoming so difficult for him as the day advanced that the smell took second place. At two in the afternoon, when the heaviness of the heat should have melted them, Pedro Vicario couldn't stay there lying on the bed, but the same weariness prevented him from standing. The pain in his groin had reached his throat, his urine was shut off, and he suffered the frightful certainty that he wouldn't sleep ever again for the rest of his life. "I was awake for eleven months," he told me, and I knew him well enough to know that it was true. He couldn't eat any lunch. Pablo Vicario, for his part, ate a little bit of everything they brought him, and fifteen minutes later unloosed a pestilential diarrhea. At six in the afternoon, while they were performing the autopsy on Santiago Nasar's corpse, the mayor was summoned urgently because Pedro Vicario was convinced that his brother had been poisoned. "He was turning into water right in front of me," Pedro Vicario told me, "and we couldn't get rid of the idea that it was some trick of the Turks." Up till then he'd overflowed the portable latrine twice and the guard on watch had taken him to the town hall washroom another six times. There Colonel Aponte found him, in the doorless toilet boxed in by the guard, and pouring out water so fluently that it wasn't too absurd to think about poison. But they put the idea aside immediately when it was established that he had only drunk the water and eaten the food sent by Pura Vicario. Nonetheless, the mayor was so impressed that he had the prisoners taken to his house under a special guard until the investigating judge came and transferred them to the panoptic prison in Riohacha.

The twins' fear was in response to the mood in the streets. Revenge by the Arabs wasn't dismissed, but no one, except the Vicario brothers, had thought of poison. It was supposed, rather, that they would wait for nightfall in order to pour gasoline through the skylight and burn up the prisoners in their cell. But even that was too easy a supposition. The Arabs comprised a community of peaceful immigrants who had settled at the beginning of the century in Caribbean towns, even in the poorest and most remote, and there they remained, selling colored cloth and bazaar trinkets. They were clannish, hardworking, and Catholic. They married among themselves, imported their wheat, raised lambs in their yards, and grew oregano and eggplants, and playing cards was their only driving passion. The older ones continued speaking the rustic Arabic they had brought from their homeland, and they maintained it intact in the family down to the second generation, but those of the third, with the exception of Santiago Nasar, listened to their parents in Arabic and answered them in Spanish. So it was inconceivable that they would suddenly abandon their pastoral spirit to avenge a death for which we all could have been to blame. On the other hand, no one thought about reprisals from Plácida Linero's family, who had been powerful and fighting people until their fortune ran out, and had bred more than two barroom killers who had been preserved by the salt of their name.

Colonel Aponte, worried by the rumors, visited the Arabs family by family and that time, at least, drew a correct conclusion. He found them perplexed and sad, with signs of mourning on their altars, and some of them sitting on the ground and wailing, but none harbored ideas of vengeance. The reaction that morning had grown out of the heat of the crime, and even the very leaders admitted that in no case would it have gone beyond a beating. Furthermore, it was Susana Abdala, the centenarian matriarch, who recommended the prodigious infusion of passion flowers and absinthe that dried up Pablo Vicario's diarrhea and unleashed at the same time his brother's florid flow. Pedro Vicario then fell into an insomniac drowsiness and his recovered brother earned his first sleep without remorse. That was how Purísima Vicario found them at three o'clock in the morning on Tuesday when the mayor brought her to say good-bye to them.

The whole family left, even the older sisters with their husbands, on Colonel Aponte's initiative. They left without anyone's noticing, sheltered by public exhaustion, while the only survivors of that irreparable day among us who were awake were burying Santiago Nasar. They were leaving until spirits cooled off, according to the mayor's decision, but they never came back. Pura Vicario wrapped the face of the rejected daughter in a cloth so that no one would see the bruises, and she dressed her in bright red so nobody might think she was mourning her secret lover. Before leaving she asked Father Amador to confess her sons in jail, but Pedro Vicario refused, and convinced his brother that they had nothing to repent. They remained alone, and on the day of their transfer to Riohacha they had so far recovered and were so convinced that they were right that they didn't want to be taken out by night, as had happened with the family, but in broad daylight and with their faces showing. Poncio Vicario, the father, died a short time later. "His moral pain carried him off," Angela Vicario told me. When the twins were absolved, they remained in Riohacha, only a day's trip from Manaure, where the family was living. Prudencia Cotes went there to marry Pablo Vicario, who learned to work with precious metals in his father's shop and came to be an elegant goldsmith. Pedro Vicario, without love or a job, reenlisted in the armed forces three years later, earned his first sergeant's stripes, and one fine morning his patrol went into guerrilla territory singing whorehouse songs and was never heard of again.

For the immense majority of people there was only one victim: Bayardo San Román. They took it for granted that the other actors in the tragedy had been fulfilling with dignity, and even with a certain grandeur, their part of the destiny that life had assigned them. Santiago Nasar had expiated the insult, the brothers Vicario had proved their status as men, and the seduced sister was in possession of her honor once more. The only one who had lost everything was Bayardo San Román: "poor Bayardo," as he was remembered over the years. Still, no one had thought of him until after the eclipse of the moon the following Saturday, when the widower Xius told the mayor that he'd seen a phosphorescent bird fluttering over his former home, and he thought it was the soul of his wife, who was going about demanding what was hers. The mayor slapped his brow, but it had nothing to do with the widower's vision.

"Shit!" he shouted. "I'd completely forgotten about that poor man!"

He went up the hill with a patrol and found the car with its top down in front of the farmhouse, and he saw a solitary light in the bedroom, but no one answered his knocks. So they broke down a side door and searched the rooms, which were lighted by the traces of the eclipse. "Things looked like they were under water," the mayor told me. Bayardo San Román was unconscious on the bed, still the way Pura Vicario had seen him early Tuesday morning, wearing his dress pants and silk shirt, but with his shoes off. There were empty bottles on the floor and many more unopened beside the bed, but not a trace of food. "He was in the last stages of ethylic intoxication," I was told by Dr. Dionisio Iguarán, who had given him emergency treatment. But he recovered in a few hours, and as soon as his mind had cleared, he threw them out of the house with the best manners he was capable of.

"Nobody fucks with me," he said. "Not even my father with his war veteran's balls."

The mayor informed General Petronio San Román of the episode, down to the last literal phrase, in an alarming telegram. General San Román must have followed his son's wishes to the letter, because he didn't come for him, but sent his wife with their daughters and two other older women who seemed to be her sisters. They came on a cargo boat, locked in mourning up to their necks because of Bayardo San Román's misfortunes, and with their hair hanging loose in grief. Before stepping onto land, they took off their shoes and went barefoot through the streets up to the hilltop in the burning dust of noon, pulling out strands of hair by the roots and wailing loudly with such high-pitched shrieks that they seemed to be shouts of joy. I watched them pass from Magdalena Oliver's balcony, and I remember thinking that distress like theirs could only be put on in order to hide other, greater shames.

Colonel Lázaro Aponte accompanied them to the house on the hill, and then Dr. Dionisio Iguarán went up on the mule he kept for emergencies. When the sun let up, two men from the town government brought Bayardo San Román down in a hammock hanging from a pole, wrapped up to his neck in a blanket and with a retinue of wailing women. Magdalena Oliver thought he was dead.

"Collons de déu!" she exclaimed. "What a waste!"

He was laid out by alcohol again, but it was hard to believe they were carrying a living person, because his right arm was dragging on the ground, and as soon as his mother put it back inside the hammock it would fall out again, so that he left a trail on the ground from the edge of the precipice to the deck of the boat. That was all that we had left of him: the memory of a victim.

They left the farmhouse the way it was. My brothers and I would go up to explore it on carousing nights when we were home on vacation, and each time we found fewer things of value in the abandoned rooms. Once we rescued the small valise that Angela Vicario had asked her mother for on her wedding night, but we didn't pay any great attention to it. What we discovered inside seemed to be a woman's natural items for hygiene and beauty, and I only learned their real use when Angela Vicario told me many years later which things were the old wives' artifices she had been instructed in so as to deceive her husband. It was the only trace she'd left in what had been her home as a married woman for five hours.

Years later when I came back to search out the last pieces of testimony for this chronicle, not even the embers of Yolanda Xius's happiness remained. Things had been disappearing little by little, despite Colonel Lázaro Aponte's determined vigilance, even the full-length closet with six mirrors that the master craftsmen of Mompox had had to assemble inside the house because it wouldn't fit through the door. At first the widower Xius was overjoyed, thinking that all those were the posthumous recourses of his wife in carrying off what was hers. Colonel Lázaro Aponte made fun of him. But one night it occurred to him to hold a spiritualist séance in order to clear up the mystery, and the soul of Yolanda Xius confirmed in her own handwriting that it was in fact she who was recovering the knickknacks of her happiness for her house of death. The house began to crumble. The wedding car was falling apart by the door, and finally nothing remained except its weather-rotted carcass. For many years nothing was heard again of its owner. There is a declaration by him in the brief, but it is so short and conventional that it seems to have been put together at the last minute in order to comply with an unavoidable requirement. The only time I tried to talk to him, twenty-three years later, he received me with a certain aggressiveness and refused to supply even the most insignificant fact that might clarify a little his participation in the drama. In any case, not even his family knew much more about him than we did, nor did they have the slightest idea of what he had come to do in a mislaid town, with no other apparent aim than to marry a woman he had never seen.

Of Angela Vicario, on the other hand, I was always receiving periodic news that inspired an idealized image in me. My sister the nun had been going about the upper Guajira for some time trying to convert the last idolaters, and she was in the habit of stopping and chatting with Angela in the village baked by Caribbean salt where her mother had tried to bury her alive. "Regards from your cousin," she would always tell me. My sister Margot, who also visited her during the first years, told me she had bought a solid house with a large courtyard with cross ventilation, the only problem being that on nights of high tide the toilets would back up and fish would appear flopping about in the bedrooms at dawn. Everyone who saw her during that time agreed that she was absorbed and skilled at her embroidery machine, and that by her industry she had managed to forget.

Much later, during an uncertain period when I was trying to understand something of myself by selling encyclopedias and medical books in the towns of Guajira, by chance I got as far as that Indian death village. At the window of a house that faced the sea, embroidering by machine during the hottest hour of the day, was a woman half in mourning, with steel-rimmed glasses and yellowish gray hair, and hanging above her head was a cage with a canary that didn't stop singing. When I saw her like that in the idyllic frame of the window, I refused to believe that the woman there was who I thought it was, because I couldn't bring myself to admit that life might end up resembling bad literature so much. But it was she: Angela Vicario, twenty-three years after the drama.

She treated me the same as always, like a distant cousin, and answered my questions with very good judgment and a sense of humor. She was so mature and witty that it was difficult to believe that she was the same person. What surprised me most was the way in which she'd ended up understanding her own life. After a few minutes she no longer seemed as aged to me as at first sight, but almost as young as in my memory, and she had nothing in common with the person who'd been obliged to marry without love at the age of twenty. Her mother, in her grouchy old age, received me like a difficult ghost. She refused to talk about the past, and for this chronicle I had to be satisfied with a few disconnected phrases from her conversations with my mother, and a few others rescued from my memories. She had gone beyond what was possible to make Angela Vicario die in life, but the daughter herself had brought her plans to naught because she never made any mystery out of her misfortune. On the contrary, she would recount it in all its details to anyone who wanted to hear it, except for one item that would never be cleared up: who was the real cause of her damage, and how and why, because no one believed that it had really been Santiago Nasar. They belonged to two completely different worlds. No one had ever seen them together, much less alone together. Santiago Nasar was too haughty to have noticed her: "Your cousin the booby," he would say to me when he had to mention her. Besides, as we said at that time, he was a sparrow hawk. He went about alone, just like his father, nipping the bud of any wayward virgin who began showing up in those woods, but in town no other relationship ever came to be known except for the conventional one he maintained with Flora Miguel, and the stormy one with María Alejandrina Cervantes, which drove him crazy for fourteen months. The most current version, perhaps because it was the most perverse, was that Angela Vicario was protecting someone who really loved her and she had chosen Santiago Nasar's name because she thought her brothers would never dare go up against him. I tried to get that truth out of her myself when I visited her the second time, with all my arguments in order, but she barely lifted her eyes from the embroidery to knock them down. "Don't beat it to death, cousin," she told me. "He was the one."

Everything else she told without reticence, even the disaster of her wedding night. She recounted how her friends had instructed her to get her husband drunk in bed until he passed out, to feign more embarrassment than she really

felt so he'd turn out the light, to give herself a drastic douche of alum water to fake virginity, and to stain the sheet with Mercurochrome so she could display it the following day in her bridal courtyard. Her bawds hadn't counted on two things: Bayardo San Román's exceptional resistance as a drinker, and the pure decency that

Angela Vicario carried hidden inside the stolidity her mother had imposed. "I didn't do any of what they told me," she said, "because the more I thought about it, the more I realized that it was all something dirty that shouldn't be done to anybody, much less to the poor man who had the bad luck to marry me." So she let herself get undressed openly in the lighted bedroom, safe now from all the acquired fears that had ruined her life. "It was very easy," she told me, "because I'd made up my mind to die."

The truth is that she spoke about her misfortune without any shame in order to cover up the other misfortune, the real one, that was burning in her insides. No one would even have suspected until she decided to tell me that Bayardo San Román had been in her life forever from the moment he'd brought her back home. It was a coup de grâce. "Suddenly, when Mama began to hit me, I began to remember him," she told me. The blows hurt less because she knew they were for him. She went on thinking about him with a certain surprise at herself while she was lying on the dining room couch sobbing. "I wasn't crying because of the blows or anything that had happened," she told me. "I was crying because of him." She kept on thinking about him while her mother put arnica compresses on her face, and even more when she heard the shouting in the street and the fire alarm bells in the belfry, and her mother came in to tell her she could sleep now because the worst was over.

She'd been thinking about him for a long time, without any illusions, when she had to go with her mother to get her eyes examined in the hospital at Riohacha. They stopped off on the way at the Hotel del Puerto, whose owner they knew, and Pura Vicario asked for a glass of water at the bar. She was drinking it with her back to her daughter when the latter saw her own thoughts reflected in the mirrors repeated around the room. Angela Vicario turned her head with a last breath and watched him pass by without seeing her and saw him go out of the hotel. Then she looked at her mother with her heart in shreds. Pura Vicario had finished drinking, dried her lips on her sleeve, and smiled at her from the bar with her new glasses. In that smile, for the first time since her birth, Angela Vicario saw her as she was: a poor woman devoted to the cult of her defects. "Shit," she said to herself. She was so upset that she spent the whole trip back home singing aloud, and she threw herself on her bed to weep for three days.

She was reborn. "I went crazy over him," she told me, "out of my mind." She only had to close her eyes to see him, she heard him breathing in the sea, the blaze of his body in bed would awaken her at midnight. Toward the end of that week, unable to get a moment's rest, she wrote him the first letter. It was a conventional missive, in which she told him that she'd seen him come out of the hotel, and that she would have liked it if he had seen her. She waited in vain for a reply. At the end of two months, tired of waiting, she sent him another letter in the same oblique style as the previous one, whose only aim seemed to be to reproach him for his lack of courtesy. Six months later she had written six letters with no reply, but she comforted herself with the certainty that he was getting them.

Mistress of her fate for the first time, Angela Vicario then discovered that hate and love are reciprocal passions. The more letters she sent the more the coals of her fever burned, but the happy rancor she felt for her mother also heated up. "Just seeing her would turn my stomach," she told me, "but I couldn't see her without remembering him." Her life as a rejected wife continued on, simple as that of an old maid, still doing machine embroidery with her friends just as before she had made cloth tulips and paper birds, but when her mother went to bed she would stay in the room until dawn writing letters with no future. She became lucid, overbearing, mistress of her own free will, and she became a virgin again just for him, and she recognized no other authority than her own nor any other service than that of her obsession.

She wrote a weekly letter for over half a lifetime. "Sometimes I couldn't think of what to say," she told me, dying with laughter, "but it was enough for me to know that he was getting them." At first they were a fiancée's notes, then they were little messages from a secret lover, perfumed cards from a furtive sweetheart, business papers, love documents, and lastly they were the indignant letters of an abandoned wife who invented cruel illnesses to make him return. One night, in a good mood, she spilled the inkwell over the finished letter and instead of tearing it up she added a postscript: "As proof of my love I send you my tears." On occasion, tired of weeping, she would make fun of her own madness. Six times the post-mistresses were changed and six times she wore their complicity. The only thing that didn't occur to her was to give up. Nevertheless, he seemed insensible to her delirium; it was like writing to nobody.

Early one windy morning in the tenth year, she was awakened by the certainty that he was naked in her bed. Then she wrote him a feverish letter, twenty pages long, in which without shame she let out the bitter truths that she had carried rotting in her heart ever since that ill-fated night. She spoke to him of the eternal scars he had left on her body, the salt of his tongue, the fiery furrow of his African tool. On Friday she gave it to the postmistress who came Friday afternoons to embroider with her and pick up the letters, and she was convinced that that final alleviation would be the end of her agony. But there was no reply. From then on she was no longer conscious of what she wrote nor to whom she was really writing, but she kept on without quarter for seventeen years.

Halfway through one August day, while she was embroidering with her friends, she heard someone coming to the door. She didn't have to look to see who it was. "He was fat and was beginning to lose his hair, and he already needed glasses to see things close by," she told me. "But it was him, God damn it, it was him!" She was frightened because she knew he was seeing her just as diminished as she saw him, and she didn't think he had as much love inside as she to bear up under it. His shirt was soaked in sweat, as she had seen him the first time at the fair, and he was wearing the same belt, and carrying the same unstitched leather saddlebags with silver decorations. Bayardo San Román took a step forward, unconcerned about the other astonished embroiderers, and laid his saddlebags on the sewing machine.

"Well," he said, "here I am."

He was carrying a suitcase with clothing in order to stay and another just like it with almost two thousand letters that she had written him. They were arranged by date in bundles tied with colored ribbons, and they were all unopened.

For years we couldn't talk about anything else. Our daily conduct, dominated then by so many linear habits, had suddenly begun to spin around a single common anxiety. The cocks of dawn would catch us trying to give order to the chain of many chance events that had made absurdity possible, and it was obvious that we weren't doing it from an urge to clear up mysteries but because none of us could go on living without an exact knowledge of the place and the mission assigned to us by fate.

Many never got to know. Cristo Bedoya, who went on to become a surgeon of renown, never managed to explain to himself why he gave in to the impulse to spend two hours at his grandparents' house until the bishop came instead of going to rest at his parents', who had been waiting for him since dawn to warn him.

But most of those who could have done something to prevent the crime and did not consoled themselves with the pretext that affairs of honor are sacred monopolies, giving access only to those who are part of the drama. "Honor is love," I heard my mother say. Hortensia Baute, whose only participation was having seen two bloody knives that weren't bloody yet, felt so affected by the hallucination that she fell into a penitential crisis, and one day, unable to stand it any longer, she ran out naked into the street. Flora Miguel, Santiago Nasar's fiancée, ran away out of spite with a lieutenant of the border patrol, who prostituted her among the rubber workers on the Vichada. Aura Villeros, the midwife who had helped bring three generations into the world, suffered a spasm of the bladder when she heard the news and to the day of her death had to use a catheter in order to urinate. Don Rogelio de la Flor, Clotilde Armenta's good husband, who was a marvel of vitality at the age of eighty-six, got up for the last time to see how they had hewn Santiago Nasar to bits against the locked door of his own house, and he didn't survive the shock. Plácida Linero had locked that door at the last moment, but with the passage of time she freed herself from blame. "I locked it because

Divina Flor had sworn to me that she'd seen my son come in," she told me, "and it wasn't true." On the other hand, she never forgave herself for having mixed up the magnificent augury of trees with the unlucky one of birds, and she succumbed to the pernicious habit of her time of chewing pepper cress seeds.

Twelve days after the crime, the investigating magistrate came upon a town that was an open wound. In the squalid wooden office in the town hall, drinking pot coffee laced with cane liquor against the mirages of the heat, he had to ask for troop reinforcements to control the crowd that was pouring in to testify without having been summoned, everyone eager to show off his own important role in the drama. The magistrate was newly graduated and still wore his black linen law school suit and the gold ring with the emblem of his degree, and he had the airs and the lyricism of a happy new parent. But I never discovered his name. Everything we know about his character has been learned from the brief, which several people helped me look for twenty years later in the Palace of Justice in Riohacha. There was no classification of files whatever, and more than a century of cases were piled up on the floor of the decrepit colonial building that had been Sir Francis Drake's headquarters for two days. The ground floor would be flooded by high tides and the unbound volumes floated about the deserted offices. I searched many times with the water up to my ankles in that lagoon of lost causes, and after five years rummaging around only chance let me rescue some 322 pages filched from the more than 500 that the brief must have contained.

The judge's name didn't appear on any of them, but it was obvious that he was a man burning with the fever of literature. He had doubtless read the Spanish classics and a few Latin ones, and he was quite familiar with Nietzsche, who was the fashionable author among magistrates of his time. The marginal notes, and not just because of the color of the ink, seemed to be written in blood. He was so perplexed by the enigma that fate had touched him with, that he kept falling into lyrical distractions that ran contrary to the rigor of his profession. Most of all, he never thought it legitimate that life should make use of so many coincidences forbidden literature, so that there should be the untrammeled fulfillment of a death so clearly foretold.

Nevertheless, what had alarmed him most at the conclusion of his excessive diligence was not having found a single clue, not even the most improbable, that Santiago Nasar had been the cause of the wrong. The friends of Angela Vicario who had been her accomplices in the deception went on saying for a long time that she had shared her secret with them before the wedding, but that she hadn't revealed any name. In the brief, they declared: "She told us about the miracle but not the saint." Angela Vicario, for her part, wouldn't budge. When the investigating magistrate asked her with his oblique style if she knew who the decedent Santiago Nasar was, she answered him impassively:

"He was my perpetrator."

That's the way she swears in the brief, but with no further precision of either how or where. During the trial, which lasted only three days, the representative of the people put his greatest effort into the weakness of that charge. Such was the perplexity of the investigating magistrate over the lack of proof against Santiago Nasar that his good work at times seemed ruined by disillusionment. On folio 416, in his own handwriting and with the druggist's red ink, he wrote a marginal note: *Give me a prejudice and I will move the world*. Under that paraphrase of discouragement, in a merry sketch with the same blood ink, he drew a heart pierced by an arrow. For him, just as for Santiago Nasar's closest friends, the victim's very behavior during his last hours was overwhelming proof of his innocence.

On the morning of his death, in fact, Santiago Nasar hadn't had a moment of doubt, in spite of the fact that he knew very well what the price of the insult imputed to him was. He was aware of the prudish disposition of his world, and he must have understood that the twins' simple nature was incapable of resisting an insult. No one knew Bayardo San Román very well, but Santiago Nasar knew him well enough to know that underneath his worldly airs he was as subject as anyone else to his native prejudices. So the murdered man's refusal to worry could have been suicide. Besides, when he finally learned at the last moment that the Vicario brothers were waiting for him to kill him, his reaction was not one of panic, as has so often been said, but rather the bewilderment of innocence.

My personal impression is that he died without understanding his death. After he'd promised my sister Margot that he would come and have breakfast at our house, Cristo Bedoya took him by the arm as they strolled along the dock and both seemed so unconcerned that they gave rise to false impressions. "They were both going along so contentedly," Meme Loiza told me, "that I gave thanks to God, because I thought the matter had been cleared up." Not everybody loved Santiago Nasar so much, of course. Polo Carrillo, the owner of the electric plant, thought that his serenity wasn't innocence but cynicism.

"He thought that his money made him untouchable," he told me. Fausta López, his wife, commented: "Just like all Turks." Indalecio Pardo had just passed by Clotilde Armenta's store and the twins had told him that as soon as the bishop left, they were going to kill Santiago Nasar. Like so many others, he thought these were the usual fantasies of very early risers, but Clotilde Armenta made him see that it was true, and she asked him to get to Santiago Nasar and warn him.

"Don't bother," Pedro Vicario told him. "No matter what, he's as good as dead already."

It was too obvious a challenge: the twins knew the bonds between Indalecio Pardo and Santiago Nasar, and they must have thought that he was just the right person to stop the crime without bringing any shame on them. But Indalecio found Santiago Nasar being led by the arm by Cristo Bedoya among the groups that were leaving the docks, and he didn't dare warn him. "I lost my nerve," he told me. He gave each one a pat on the back and let them go their way. They scarcely noticed, because they were still taken up with the costs of the wedding.

The people were breaking up and heading toward the square the same way they were. It was a thick crowd, but Escolástica Cisneros thought she noticed that the two friends were walking in the center of it without any difficulty, inside an empty circle, because everyone knew that Santiago Nasar was about to die and they didn't dare touch him. Cristo Bedoya also remembered a strange attitude toward them. "They were looking at us as if we had our faces painted," he told me. Also, Sara Noriega was opening her shoe store at the moment they passed and she was frightened at Santiago Nasar's paleness. But he calmed her down.

"You can imagine, Missy Sara," he told her without stopping, "with this hangover!"

Celeste Dangond was sitting in his pajamas by the door of his house, mocking those who had gone to greet the bishop, and he invited Santiago Nasar to have some coffee. "It was in order to gain some time to think," he told me. But Santiago Nasar answered that he was in a hurry to change clothes to have breakfast with my sister. "I got all mixed up," Celeste Dangond told me, "because it suddenly seemed to me that they couldn't be killing him if he was so sure of what he was going to do." Yamil Shaium was the only one who did what he had proposed doing. As soon as he heard the rumor, he went out to the door of his dry goods store and waited for Santiago Nasar so he could warn him. He was one of the last Arabs who had come with Ibrahim Nasar, had been his partner in cards until his death, and was still the hereditary counselor of the family. No one had as much authority as he to talk to Santiago Nasar. Nevertheless, he thought that if the rumor was baseless it would alarm him unnecessarily, and he preferred to consult first with Cristo Bedoya in case the latter was better informed. He called to him as he went by. Cristo Bedoya gave a pat on the back to Santiago Nasar, who was already at the corner of the square, and answered Yamil Shaium's call. "See you Saturday," he told him.

Santiago Nasar didn't reply, but said something in Arabic to Yamil Shaium, and the latter answered him, also in Arabic, twisting with laughter. "It was a play on words we always had fun with," Yamil Shaium told me. Without stopping, Santiago Nasar waved good-bye to both of them and turned the corner of the square. It was the last time they saw him.

Cristo Bedoya only took the time to grasp Yamil Shaium's information before he ran out of the store to catch Santiago Nasar. He'd seen him turn the corner, but he couldn't find him

among the groups that were beginning to break up on the square. Several people he asked gave him the same answer.

"I just saw him with you."

It seemed impossible that he could have reached home in such a short time, but just in case, he went in to ask about him since he found the front door unbarred and ajar. He went in without seeing the paper on the floor. He passed through the shadowy living room, trying not to make any noise, because it was still too early for visitors, but the dogs became aroused at the back of the house and came out to meet him. He calmed them down with his keys as he'd learned from their master, and went on toward the kitchen, with them following. On the veranda he came upon Divina Flor, who was carrying a pail of water and a rag to clean the floor in the living room. She assured him that Santiago Nasar hadn't returned. Victoria Guzmán had just put the rabbit stew on the stove when he entered the kitchen. She understood immediately. "His heart was in his mouth," she told me. Cristo Bedoya asked her if Santiago Nasar was home, and she answered him with feigned innocence that he still hadn't come in to go to sleep.

"It's serious," Cristo Bedoya told her. "They're looking for him to kill him."

Victoria Guzmán forgot her innocence.

"Those poor boys won't kill anybody," she said.

"They've been drinking since Saturday," Cristo Bedoya said.

"That's just it," she replied. "There's no drunk in the world who'll eat his own crap."

Cristo Bedoya went back to the living room, where Divina Flor had just opened the windows. "Of course it wasn't raining," Cristo Bedoya told me. "It was just going on seven and a golden sun was already coming through the windows." He asked Divina Flor again if she was sure that Santiago Nasar hadn't come in through the living room door. She wasn't as sure then as the first time. He asked her about Plácida Linero, and she answered that just a moment before she'd put her coffee on the night table, but she hadn't awakened her. That's the way it always was: Plácida Linero would wake up at seven, have her coffee, and come down to give instructions for lunch. Cristo Bedoya looked at the clock: it was six fifty-six. Then he climbed up to the second floor to make sure that Santiago Nasar hadn't come in.

The bedroom was locked from the inside, because Santiago Nasar had gone out through his mother's bedroom. Cristo Bedoya not only knew the house as well as his own, but was so much at home with the family that he pushed open the door to Plácida Linero's bedroom and went from there into the adjoining one. A beam of dusty light was coming in through the skylight, and the beautiful woman asleep on her side in the hammock, her bride's hand on her cheek, had an unreal look. "It was like an apparition," Cristo Bedoya told me. He looked at her for an instant, fascinated by her beauty, and then he crossed the room in silence, passed by the bathroom, and proceeded into Santiago Nasar's bedroom. The bed was still made, and on the chair, well-pressed, were his riding clothes, and on top of the clothes his horseman's hat, and on the floor his boots beside their spurs. On the night table, Santiago Nasar's wristwatch said six fifty-eight. "Suddenly I thought that he'd come back so that he could go out armed," Cristo Bedoya told me. But he found the Magnum in the drawer of the night table. "I'd never shot a gun," Cristo Bedoya told me, "but I decided to take the revolver and bring it to Santiago Nasar." He stuck it in his belt, under his shirt, and only after the crime did he realize that it was unloaded. Plácida Linero appeared in the doorway with her mug of coffee just as he was closing the drawer.

"Good heavens!" she exclaimed. "You gave me a start!"

Cristo Bedoya was also startled. He saw her in the full light, wearing a dressing gown with golden larks, her hair loose, and the charm had vanished. He explained, somewhat confused, that he was looking for Santiago Nasar.

"He went to receive the bishop," Plácida Linero said.

"The bishop went right through," he said.

"I thought so," she said. "He's the son of the worst kind of mother."

She didn't go on because at that moment she realized that Cristo Bedoya didn't know what to do with his body. "I hope that God has forgiven me," Plácida Linero told me, "but he seemed so confused that it suddenly occurred to me that he'd come to rob us." She asked him what was wrong. Cristo Bedoya was aware that he was in a suspicious situation, but he didn't have the courage to reveal the truth.

"It's just that I haven't had a minute's sleep," he told her.

He left without any further explanations. "In any case," he told me, "she was always imagining that she was being robbed." In the square he ran into Father Amador, who was returning to the church with the vestments for the frustrated mass, but he didn't think he could do anything for Santiago Nasar except save his soul. He was heading toward the docks again when he heard them calling him from the door of Clotilde Armenta's store. Pedro Vicario was in the doorway, pale and haggard, his shirt open and his sleeves rolled up to the elbows, and with the naked knife in his hand. His manner was too insolent to be natural, and yet it wasn't the only final or the most visible pose that he'd assumed in the last moments so they would stop him from committing the crime.

"Cristóbal," he shouted, "tell Santiago Nasar that we're waiting for him here to kill him."

Cristo Bedoya could have done him the favor of stopping him. "If I'd known how to shoot a revolver, Santiago Nasar would be alive today," he told me. But the idea did impress him, after all he'd heard about the devastating power of an armor-plated bullet.

"I warn you. He's armed with a Magnum that can go through an engine block," he shouted.

Pedro Vicario knew it wasn't true. "He never went armed except when he wore riding clothes," he told me. But in any case, he'd foreseen the possibility that he might be armed when he made the decision to wipe his sister's honor clean.

"Dead men can't shoot," he shouted.

Then Pablo Vicario appeared in the doorway. He was as pale as his brother and he was wearing his wedding jacket and carrying his knife wrapped in the newspaper. "If it hadn't been for that," Cristo Bedoya told me, "I never would have known which of the two was which." Clotilde Armenta then appeared behind Pablo Vicario and shouted to Cristo Bedoya to hurry up, because in that faggot town only a man like him could prevent the tragedy.

Everything that happened after that is in the public domain. The people who were coming back from the docks, alerted by the shouts, began to take up positions around the square to witness the crime. Cristo Bedoya asked several people he knew if they'd seen Santiago Nasar, but no one had. At the door of the social club he ran into Colonel Lázaro Aponte and he told him what had just happened in front of Clotilde Armenta's store.

"It can't be," Colonel Aponte said, "because I told them to go home to bed."

"I just saw them with pig-killing knives," Cristo Bedoya said.

"It can't be, because I took them away from them before sending them home to bed," said the mayor. "It must be that you saw them before that."

"I saw them two minutes ago and they both

had pig-killing knives," Cristo Bedoya said.

"Oh, shit," the mayor said. "Then they must have come back with two new ones."

He promised to take care of it at once, but he went into the social club to check on a date for dominoes that night, and when he came out again the crime had already been committed. Cristo Bedoya then made his only mortal mistake: he thought that Santiago Nasar had decided at the last moment to have breakfast at our house before changing his clothes, and he went to look for him there. He hurried along the riverbank, asking everyone he passed if they'd seen him go by, but no one said he had. He wasn't alarmed, because there were other ways to get to our house. Próspera Arango, the uplander, begged him to do something for her father, who was in his death throes on the stoop of his house, immune to the bishop's fleeting blessing. "I'd seen him when I passed," my sister Margot told me, "and he already had the face of a dead man." Cristo Bedoya delayed four minutes to ascertain the sick man's condition, and promised to come back later for some emergency treatment, but he lost three minutes more helping Próspera Arango carry him into the bedroom. When he came out again he heard distant shouts and it seemed to him that rockets were being fired in the direction of the square. He tried to run but was hindered by the revolver, which was clumsily stuck in his belt. As he turned the last corner he recognized my mother from the rear as she was practically dragging her youngest son along.

"Luisa Santiaga," he shouted to her, "where's your godson?"

My mother barely turned, her face bathed in tears.

"Oh, my son," she answered, "they say he's been killed!"

That's how it was. While Cristo Bedoya had been looking for him, Santiago Nasar had gone into the house of Flora Miguel, his fiancée, just around the corner from where he'd seen him for the last time. "It didn't occur to me that he could be there," he told me, "because those people never got up before noon." The version that went around was that the whole family slept until twelve o'clock on orders from Nahir Miguel, the wise man of the community. "That's why Flora Miguel, who wasn't that young anymore, was preserved like a rose," Mercedes says. The truth is that they kept the house locked up until very late, like so many others, but they were early-rising and hard-working people. The parents of Santiago Nasar and Flora Miguel had agreed that they should get married. Santiago Nasar accepted the engagement in the bloom of his adolescence, and he was determined to fulfill it, perhaps because he had the same utilitarian concept of matrimony as his father. Flora Miguel, for her part, enjoyed a certain floral quality, but she lacked wit and judgment and had served as bridesmaid for her whole generation, so the agreement was a providential solution for her. They had an easy engagement, without formal visits or restless hearts. The wedding, postponed several times, was finally set for the following Christmas.

Flora Miguel awoke that Monday with the first bellows of the bishop's boat, and shortly thereafter she found out that the Vicario twins were waiting for Santiago Nasar to kill him. She informed my sister the nun, the only one she spoke to after the misfortune, that she didn't even remember who'd told her. "I only know that at six o'clock in the morning everybody knew it," she told her. Nevertheless, it seemed inconceivable to her that they were going to kill Santiago Nasar, but on the other hand, it occurred to her that they would force him to marry Angela Vicario in order to give her back her honor. She went through a crisis of humiliation. While half the town was waiting for the bishop, she was in her bedroom weeping with rage, and putting in order the chestful of letters that Santiago Nasar had sent her from school.

Whenever he passed by Flora Miguel's house, even if nobody was home, Santiago Nasar would scratch his keys across the window screens. That Monday she was waiting with the chest of letters in her lap. Santiago Nasar couldn't see her from the street, but she, however, saw him approaching through the screen before he scratched it with his keys.

"Come in," she told him.

No one, not even a doctor, had entered that house at six forty-five in the morning. Santiago Nasar had just left Cristo Bedoya at Yamil Shaium's store, and there were so many people hanging on his movements in the square that it was difficult to believe that no one saw him go into his fiancée's house. The investigating magistrate looked for a single person who'd seen him, and he did so with as much persistence as I, but it was impossible to find one. In folio 382 of the brief, he wrote another marginal pronouncement in red ink: *Fatality makes us invisible.* The fact is that Santiago Nasar went in through the main door, in full view of everyone, and without doing anything not to be seen. Flora Miguel was waiting for him in the parlor, green with rage, wearing one of the dresses with unfortunate ruffles that she was in the habit of putting on for memorable occasions, and she placed the chest in his hands.

"Here you are," she told him. "And I hope they kill you!"

Santiago Nasar was so perplexed that he dropped the chest and his loveless letters poured out onto the floor. He tried to catch Flora Miguel in the bedroom, but she closed the door and threw the bolt. He knocked several times, and called her in too pressing a voice for the time of day, so the whole family came in, all alarmed. Counting relatives by blood and by marriage, adults and minors, there were more than fourteen of them. The last to come was Nahir Miguel, the father, with his red beard and the Bedouin caftan he had brought from his homeland and which he always wore at home. I saw him many times and he was immense and spare, but what most impressed me was the glow of his authority.

"Flora," he called in his language. "Open the door."

He went into his daughter's bedroom while the family stared at Santiago Nasar. He was kneeling in the parlor, picking up the letters and putting them into the chest. "It looked like a penance," they told me. Nahir Miguel came out of the bedroom after a few minutes, made a signal with his hand, and the whole family disappeared.

He continued talking in Arabic to Santiago Nasar. "From the first moment I understood that he didn't have the slightest idea of what I was saying," he told me. Then he asked him outright if he knew that the Vicario brothers were looking for him to kill him. "He turned pale and lost control in such a way that it was impossible to think that he was pretending," he told me. He agreed that his manner reflected not so much fear as confusion.

"Only you can know if they're right or not," he told him. "But in any case, you've only got two paths to follow now: either you hide here, in this house which is yours, or you go out with my rifle."

"I don't understand a God-damned thing," Santiago Nasar said.

It was the only thing he managed to say, and he said it in Spanish. "He looked like a little wet bird," Nahir Miguel told me. He had to take the chest from his hands because he didn't know where to put it in order to open the door.

"It'll be two against one," he told him.

Santiago Nasar left. The people had stationed themselves on the square the way they did on parade days. They all saw him come out, and they all understood that now he knew they were going to kill him, and that he was so confused he couldn't find his way home. They say that someone shouted from a balcony: "Not that way, Turk; by the old dock." Santiago Nasar sought out the voice. Yamil Shaium shouted for him to get into his store and went to get his hunting gun, but he couldn't remember where he'd put the cartridges. They began to shout at him from every side, and Santiago Nasar went backward and forward several times, baffled by hearing so many voices at the same time. It was obvious that he was heading toward his house as if to enter through the kitchen door, but suddenly he must have realized that the main door was open.

"There he comes," said Pedro Vicario.

They'd both seen him at the same time. Pablo Vicario took off his jacket, put it on the bench, and unwrapped his knife, holding it like a scimitar. Before leaving the store, without any agreement, they both crossed themselves. Then Clotilde Armenta grabbed Pedro Vicario by the shirt and shouted to Santiago Nasar to run because they were going to kill him. It was such an urgent shout that it drowned out all the others. "At first he was startled," Clotilde Armenta told me, "because he didn't know who was shouting at him or from where." But when he saw her, he also saw Pedro Vicario, who threw her to the ground and caught up with his brother. Santiago Nasar was less than fifty yards from his house and he ran to the main door.

Five minutes before, in the kitchen, Victoria Guzmán had told Plácida Linero what everybody already knew. Plácida Linero was a woman of steady nerves, so she didn't let any sign of alarm show through. She asked Victoria Guzmán if she'd said anything to her son, and she lied honestly, since she answered that she still hadn't known anything when he came down for coffee. In the living room, where she was still scrubbing the floor, Divina Flor at the same time saw Santiago Nasar come in through the door on the square and go up the open stairs to the bedrooms. "It was a very clear vision," Divina Flor told me. "He was wearing his white suit and carrying something that I couldn't make out well in his hand, but it looked like a bouquet of roses." So when Plácida Linero asked about him, Divina Flor calmed her down.

"He went up to his room a minute ago," she told her.

Plácida Linero then saw the paper on the floor, but she didn't think to pick it up, and she only found out what it said when someone showed it to her later on during the confusion of the tragedy. Through the door she saw the Vicario brothers running toward the house with their knives out. From the place where she was standing she could see them but she couldn't see her son, who was running toward the door from a different angle. "I thought they wanted to get in to kill him inside the house," she told me. Then she ran to the door and slammed it shut. She was putting up the bar when she heard Santiago Nasar's shouts, and she heard the terrified pounding on the door, but she thought he was upstairs, insulting the Vicario brothers from the balcony in his room. She went up to help him.

Santiago Nasar only needed a few seconds to get in when the door closed. He managed to pound with his fists several times, and he turned at once to face his enemies with his bare hands. "I was scared when I saw him face on," Pablo

Vicario told me, "because he looked twice as big as he was." Santiago Nasar raised his hand to stop the first strike from Pedro Vicario, who attacked him on the right side with his knife pointed straight in.

"Sons of bitches!" he shouted.

The knife went through the palm of his right hand and then sank into his side up to the hilt. Everybody heard his cry of pain.

"Oh, mother of mine!"

Pedro Vicario pulled out his knife with his slaughterer's iron wrist and dealt him a second thrust almost in the same place. "The strange thing is that the knife kept coming out clean," Pedro Vicario declared to the investigator. "I'd given it to him at least three times and there wasn't a drop of blood." Santiago Nasar twisted after the third stab, his arms crossed over his stomach, let out the moan of a calf, and tried to turn his back to them. Pablo Vicario, who was on his left, then gave him the only stab in the back and a spurt of blood under high pressure soaked his shirt. "It smelled like him," he told me. Mortally wounded three times, Santiago Nasar turned frontward again and leaned his back against his mother's door, without the slightest resistance, as if he only wanted to help them finish killing him by his own contribution. "He didn't cry out again," Pedro Vicario told the investigator. "Just the opposite: it looked to me as if he was laughing." Then they both kept on knifing him against the door with alternate and easy stabs, floating in the dazzling backwater they had found on the other side of fear. They didn't hear the shouts of the whole town, frightened by its own crime. "I felt the way you do when you're galloping on horseback," Pablo Vicario declared. But they both suddenly woke up to reality, because they were exhausted, and yet they thought that Santiago Nasar would never fall. "Shit, cousin," Pablo Vicario told me, "you

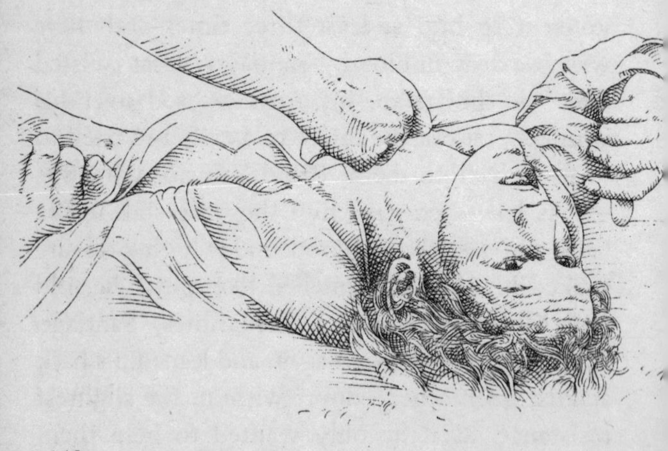

can't imagine how hard it is to kill a man!" Trying to finish it once and for all, Pedro Vicario sought his heart, but he looked for it almost in the armpit, where pigs have it. Actually, Santiago Nasar wasn't falling because they themselves were holding him up with stabs against the door. Desperate, Pablo Vicario gave him a horizontal slash on the stomach, and all his intestines exploded out. Pedro Vicario was about to do the same, but his wrist twisted with horror and he gave him a wild cut on the thigh. Santiago Nasar was still for an instant, leaning against the door, until he saw his own viscera in the sunlight, clean and blue, and he fell on his knees.

After looking and shouting for him in the bedroom, hearing other shouts that weren't hers and not knowing where they were coming from, Plácida Linero went to the window facing the square and saw the Vicario twins running toward the church. Hot in pursuit was Yamil Shaium with his jaguar gun and some other unarmed Arabs, and Plácida Linero thought the danger had passed. Then she went out onto the bedroom balcony and saw Santiago Nasar in front of the door, face down in the dust, trying to rise up out of his own blood. He stood up, leaning to one side, and started to walk in a state of hallucination, holding his hanging intestines in his hands.

He walked more than a hundred yards, completely around the house, and went in through the kitchen door. He still had enough lucidity not to go along the street, it was the longest way, but by way of the house next door. Poncho Lanao, his wife, and their five children hadn't known what had just happened twenty paces from their door. "We heard the shouting," the wife told me, "but we thought it was part of the bishop's festival." They were sitting down to breakfast when they saw Santiago Nasar enter, soaked in blood and carrying the roots of his entrails in his hands. Poncho Lanao told me: "What I'll never forget was the terrible smell of shit." But Argénida Lanao, the oldest daughter, said that Santiago Nasar walked with his usual good bearing, measuring his steps well, and that his Saracen face with its dashing ringlets was handsomer than ever. As he passed by the table he smiled at them and continued through the bedrooms to the rear door of the house. "We were paralyzed with fright," Argénida Lanao told me. My aunt, Wenefrida Márquez, was scaling a shad in her yard on the other side of the river when she saw him go down the steps of the old dock, looking for his way home with a firm step.

"Santiago, my son," she shouted to him, "what has happened to you?"

"They've killed me, Wene child," he said.

He stumbled on the last step, but he got up at once. "He even took care to brush off the dirt that was stuck to his guts," my Aunt Wene told me. Then he went into his house through the back door that had been open since six and fell on his face in the kitchen.

About the Author

Gabriel García Márquez was born in Aracataca, Colombia, in 1928, the eldest of sixteen children; he has lived mostly in Mexico and Europe. He attended the University of Bogotá, and later worked as a reporter for the Colombian newspaper *El Espectador* and as a foreign correspondent in Rome, Paris, Barcelona, Caracas, and New York. In 1971 he was awarded an honorary doctorate of letters by Columbia University. His most celebrated novel, *One Hundred Years of Solitude*, has sold more than 10 million copies in thirty-two languages. Other works of fiction include *No One Writes to the Colonel and Other Stories, The Autumn of the Patriarch, Leaf Storm and Other Stories, In Evil Hour, Innocent Erendira and Other Stories, Love In the Time of Cholera,* and *The General in His Labyrinth.* He is the winner of the 1982 Nobel Prize for Literature.

About the Illustrator

Paul Giovanopoulos, born in Greece, came to America in 1956. He is a Gold Medal recipient from the Society of Illustrators. His work is displayed in the permanent collection of 24 museums. He paints and illustrates in New York, where he lives with his wife, Jami.